CASTLE MACNAB

CASTLE MACNAB

Robert J. Harris was born in Dundee and studied at the University of St Andrews where he graduated with a first class honours degree in Latin. He is the designer of the bestselling fantasy board game Talisman and has written numerous books including *Leonardo and the Death Machine*, *Will Shakespeare and the Pirate's Fire*, and more recently The Artie Conan Doyle Mysteries, a series featuring the youthful adventures of the creator of Sherlock Holmes. His first Richard Hannay novel, *The Thirty-One Kings*, was acclaimed by critics and readers alike and was listed by *The Scotsman* as one of the fifty best books of 2017. He lives in St Andrews with his wife Debby.

ROBERT J. HARRIS
CASTLE MACNAB

Richard Hannay Returns

Polygon

First published in Great Britain in 2018 by Polygon, an imprint of Birlinn Ltd.
This paperback edition published in 2019 by Polygon.

Birlinn Ltd
West Newington House
10 Newington Road
Edinburgh
EH9 1QS

www.polygonbooks.co.uk

1

ISBN 978 1 84697 478 6
eBook ISBN 978 1 78885 060 5

Design and typesetting by Studio Monachino
Printed and bound by Clays Ltd, Elcograf S.p.A.

To Steve – the spirit of John Macnab lives on!

CONTENTS

PART THREE: CASTLE MACNAB

Since recounting my escapades with the Black Stone shortly before the Great War, I have fallen into the habit of writing up my reminiscences. This particular adventure involved a number of my friends and I have made so bold as to relate their exploits based upon the first-hand accounts they reported to me.

However, for reasons of political sensitivity, this tale must be kept a close secret until such time as the events reported have lost the power to shock, embarrass or offend.

RICHARD HANNAY

PROLOGUE

THE EXILE

'The Lord also spake unto Joshua, saying, ... Appoint out for you cities of refuge, ...

'And when he that doth flee unto one of those cities shall stand at the entering of the gate of the city, and shall declare his cause in the ears of the elders of that city, they shall take him in . . . and give him a place, that he may dwell among them.

'And if the avenger of blood pursue after him, then they shall not deliver the slayer up into his hand.'

JOSHUA: XX 1–5

Doorn House, Holland, September 192–

The house at Doorn was a very pleasant prison, but it was no less a prison for its comfortably appointed apartments and its colourful, scented gardens. When the Exile first arrived in Holland in November of 1918 he had been granted sanctuary in the castle of Amerongen. That had been much more to his taste. There it had been easy to persuade himself that the castle's high walls and double moat were intended to provide him with security and keep the curious at bay, rather than to form the limits of his new, heavily restricted world.

But it chafed him to rely on the goodwill of the Bentinck family who had opened their doors to him. He eventually made use of his substantial coffers to purchase a house in nearby Doorn and have it refurbished to his own imperial tastes. From the outside it merely resembled the country retreat of a moderately successful merchant, but the Exile had added a number of rooms as well as overseeing the installation of electric lights, central heating and the most modern cooking facilities available. He had also supervised the construction of a spacious entrance hall dominated by a magnificent staircase of white Silesian marble shipped in from the royal castle in Berlin.

Today, however, neither these walls nor this flat country would contain him.

He awoke well before sunrise, even earlier than was his usual habit. He sprang from his bed with an excitement he had not felt in some time and threw open the curtains. Outside, the close-clipped lawns were heavy with dew under a cloudy sky and the poplars in the neighbouring park were half veiled in mist. The air was cool and still, the silence unbroken except by a single cock crow from a distant farmyard.

A light tap at the door announced the arrival of Hans, his faithful valet of many years, who had been instructed to advance the usual morning schedule. Hans was the only person in the house who still insisted on wearing his waxed moustache in the old upturned way, like a true Prussian.

'Good morning, Your Majesty,' he greeted his master. 'You slept well?'

'Never better, Hans,' the Exile assured him. 'You may draw my bath.'

Hans attended to his duties with his habitual brisk deference, laying out a freshly laundered set of clothes while his master completed his morning ablutions.

Half an hour later, the Exile emerged from his room dressed in a well-cut travelling suit of grey serge and comfortable leather walking shoes. He moved quietly down the upper hallway past the bedchamber of his new wife, twenty-eight years his junior. Though she was privy to the day's plan, he had urged her to keep to her usual routine, sleeping on until a maid entered with a tray of orange juice, sweet pastries and coffee.

The Exile walked with dignity down the marble stairs and paused before a life-sized portrait of himself in full naval uniform which had been painted some twenty years before. That uniform, like most of his clothes, right down to his handkerchiefs, had been looted from his palace when he made his retreat – he would not call it a flight – to Holland.

It was one of several paintings he had brought out of storage in Germany to be hung here in Doorn, along with a score of smaller works of art – miniatures and statuettes – depicting him on horseback or seated upon a throne. For the first few years here he had been too cautious to decorate the house with such images, but presently he felt the need to gaze upon his former glory, reminding himself that he was still that man from whom greatness had been unjustly stolen. The game, however, was not yet over, and he had a few cards left to play, as recent visitors from the homeland had reminded him.

Entering his study, the Exile seated himself at the broad mahogany table by the window. Crowded with mementos, the room had the air of a sanctuary. Here were the maps he had pored over so often, re-enacting in his mind those old battles, weighing a triumph here against a setback there. Time and again he had sought out some bright chink, some moment of advantage where the tide of conflict might have been turned into a victory. Such a victory would not only have preserved his throne, but have caused him to be lauded for generations yet to come as the saviour of his people and the man who brought the squabbling nations of Europe to heel under one wise and benevolent rule.

Hans drifted in with the breakfast tray, then left his master alone with the grilled sole and two poached eggs. After picking distractedly at the meal, the Exile swallowed a single cup of coffee and pushed the dishes aside. He stepped out into the hallway where Hans waited to dress him for the morning walk that was an inflexible part of his daily routine.

His favourite coat was of heavy wool, cut in the style of a military greatcoat. When Hans helped him into it, the weight of it sat well on his shoulders. Catching his reflection in a nearby mirror, he was gratified to see himself transformed from a mild country squire into a man who once commanded massed ranks of cold steel and hot blood.

A dark grey Homburg trimmed with a black cock's feather completed his ensemble. Taking leave of his valet, he marched outside and descended the broad front steps.

The light was now spreading in a silver sheen across the sky. Moving away from the house, he passed a waist-high stack of freshly chopped firewood, the result of his own labours. On any given day he could be found among the trees in the park, his shirt loose, without collar or tie, energetically setting to work with a well-sharpened axe. It was a continuation of the long-standing physical regimen by which he had overcome the infirmity of his withered left arm, the result of a difficult birth he had been lucky to survive.

In his youth it was thought that he would never be able to hold a rifle, but with strenuous effort and coaching he had become an accomplished marksman. Likewise, many doubted he would ever be able to ride, hampered by such an infirmity, but he knew what was required of a monarch, so through a combination of expert training and sheer willpower he had mastered horsemanship.

As a result of such challenges, in spite of the blessings of wealth and privilege, which were his by right, he knew what it was to struggle, to overcome the hardships inflicted by the random cruelties of fate. Even now, in his sixty-fifth year, he enjoyed a vigour that would have been the envy of many a younger man.

After completing a circuit of the rose garden, he directed his steps towards the ornamental pond he had constructed at the request of his first wife, his dear Dona. She had died before it was finished, having never fully recovered from the shock of their downfall, but he insisted it be completed as a memorial. It reminded him of her quiet, reassuring placidity, which now he missed so much. Hermine, his new bride of eighteen months, was much more demanding.

Several Hook Bill ducks were gathered at the pond, some dabbling in the water, others squatting on the bank. When the Exile appeared, they clamoured about his feet. Smiling indulgently, he reached into his pocket for the bag of breadcrumbs Hans had provided, and tossed them by the handful to the grateful birds. This simple ritual brought back memories of better days when he would fling a scattering of coins into the crowd as his state carriage pulled away from some public appearance.

When the bag was empty, he returned to the house by way of the main drive to find a familiar bicycle parked outside. It was the property of his young adjutant, Captain Sigurd von Ilsemann, who lived in nearby Amerongen with his Dutch bride, the lovely Elizabeth Bentinck. Ilsemann himself was waiting in the front hall. He greeted the Exile with a crisp salute and reported, 'All is ready, Your Majesty.'

Like his master, he was dressed for travelling, and there was a high-strung air of excitement about him.

The Exile raised an eyebrow. 'The car?'

'Parked around the back. Our luggage has been loaded.'

'You have confirmed our sea transport?'

'Yes,' the young captain replied. 'The schooner *Minerva* is just waiting for us beyond Antwerp and Baron von Hilderling will meet us there. His man Kurbin is already in Scotland and arranging transport and accommodation.'

The Exile paused briefly to savour the moment. 'That is good, Ilsemann. You have done well.'

A shadow crossed the floor, cast from above. Turning, the Exile was surprised to see his wife descending the broad staircase from the upper levels of the house. She had tied a robe of lavishly embroidered Chinese silk around her nightdress and her hair was decorously tucked up under her sleeping cap. When she reached the bottom of the stairs she glided towards them, her satin slippers making no sound on the marble floor.

'Empress,' Ilsemann greeted her with a bow. He knew she had no right to the title, but she insisted upon it, and everyone at Doorn House knew it was unwise to displease her.

Hermine ignored him. Eyes fixed on her husband, she halted within an arm's length of him. 'I had a bad dream last night,' she informed him, her tone almost reproachful. 'One to do with you becoming lost in a dangerous forest with wild beasts on every side.'

Reaching out, the Exile placed his hands on her shoulders and smiled indulgently. 'Ah, you even dream like Caesar's wife. Cast it aside. We cannot be ruled by the phantoms of the night when the bright day beckons.'

Hermine shivered slightly. 'I know, but you are taking such a risk. And for what – a jaunt?'

The Exile made haste to reassure her. 'My dear, you must not fret yourself. A few days in open hill country will do me a world of good. When I return you will see a flush in my cheek and a spring in my step that will lighten your heart as much as my own.'

'But to go there, to the land of your enemies . . .'

'*Former* enemies,' he corrected her. 'We are at peace now, and I am but a private man desirous of a modest amount of recreation.'

'Should you be recognised, what protection would you have?'

The Exile conjured up a laugh that was intended to sound carefree. 'Those Scottish Highlands were cleared of people long ago. They have been replaced by sheep, and from sheep I have nothing to fear. Besides, the good captain will be with me.'

Seeing that Hermine was about to speak again, he placed a finger firmly upon her lips. 'No, no, my will is unbending in this. Your champion must go out into the world, perhaps to return with a prize – freshly shot venison or a brace of plump grouse. Yes, instruct cook to be ready to prepare a banquet of game.'

He kissed her lightly on the brow then turned to see Ilsemann opening the door for him. It began to drizzle as they walked around the house to where the Daimler awaited with Walther, the Exile's aging chauffeur, at the wheel.

'Your wife is right to be concerned,' Ilsemann observed with a frown. 'If she learned that this was no mere holiday, she would know what the hazards truly are.'

His master gave a decisive shake of the head. 'Even if nothing more comes of it than a few days of hunting, that in itself would be worth the hazard, Sigurd. You know how suffocating my life is here. No shooting, no riding, no medals, no uniform, nothing that might remind anyone of my regal past. For a few days at least, I will be free of that constraint.'

The two men climbed into the back of the car and the chauffeur started the vehicle. At the end of the driveway, two disinterested Dutch guards opened the gate and waved them on their way. Tours in the local countryside were one of the Exile's few pleasures, and the guards were used to his frequent comings and goings. Their job, after all, was not to contain him, but to keep sightseers away and deter anyone who might wish him harm.

'You recall your instructions, Walther?' the Exile prompted as they headed northward at a cautious speed worthy of their aged driver.

'At Zuylestein you will transfer to a different car.' The chauffeur cleared his throat unhappily. 'I wish I were going with you, Your Majesty.'

The Exile spoke sternly. 'No, Walther, you must return in the afternoon when the guards have changed. Your story will be that I am indoors and you have been out to fetch petrol. Remember, Dr Haehne and the empress will tell everyone that I have retired to my bed ill and am not to be disturbed by anyone but the two of them.'

'Yes, I know, Your Majesty,' the glum old man responded. 'And Captain von Ilsemann has gone to visit relatives in the Fatherland.'

'Good, good.' The Exile clapped his hands on his knees and gazed through the rain-spattered window at the passing landscape. A smile touched his lips as he addressed his adjutant. 'I have a glorious feeling, my friend, that destiny is not done with me yet.'

PART ONE

A GAME OF KINGS

1

BENEATH THE VISITING MOON

Rushforth Lodge nestled comfortably into the folded hills of Denroy, as if that grassy shelf had been moulded by a gigantic yet kindly hand to provide a resting place for man amidst the harsh crags and thick forests. Behind the house a stony escarpment rose sharply, forming a rugged bulwark against the storms that all too often came sweeping in from the west. In front of the house the land fell away in a series of wooded terraces to the bank of a narrow, racing stream.

On this September evening the piping of curlews from the rocky overhang haunted the air like an enchantment, conjuring a pink sunset out of the hard blue sky. The lodge and its outbuildings had long ago spread to the very edge of the drop, and now exhibited a degree of dilapidation that suggested a project long abandoned. Yet the stream of peaty smoke issuing from the crooked chimney indicated warmth and good company inside.

And indeed there was. Three gentlemen rested at their leisure before the broad fireplace, each ensconced in a worn leather armchair, a bottle of fifteen-year-old Islay on a table between them surrounded by a litter of glasses and smoking paraphernalia. A genial silence presided over the room, broken only by the crackle of burning peat in the hearth. The men's attitude of satisfied relaxation bespoke a day of welcome exertion, and also an easy comfort in each other's company such as only comes from the particular friendship that stretches back to the innocent mischief of boyhood.

The tallest and darkest of the three, Lord Lamancha, had no connection whatever with the haunts of Don Quixote, though the coincidence of names certainly amused him. In his case it was derived from a shieling on the Liddesdale estate ruled over by his father the marquis. However, neither the Borders nor these Highland glens of Wester Ross were the usual environs of Charles Lamancha. He was a denizen of the cabinet offices and closeted clubs of Parliament, where he was to be found negotiating the intricate policies of a delicately balanced government.

With his black moustache and pointed chin, he resembled a Hispanic nobleman recently returned from the conquest of the New World. Friends and acquaintances often joked that he would be more at home on the deck of a pirate ship than on the floor of the Commons. No one doubted that in such a case the privateers under his command would willingly plunge into the heart of the Inferno if he chose to set such a course. The almost unconscious masterfulness of his nature led some to see him as a future leader of his country, though this was a prospect he was quick to dismiss with a mocking laugh and an airy wave of his cigar.

John Palliser-Yeates was of an altogether more practical disposition. His rounded shoulders and occasionally bullish stance were reminders that he had in his youth set crowds cheering his energetic deeds on the rugby field. Once he had the ball in his hands, it was a brave man who stood in the way of his head-down charge for the touch line. Now, he presided over a major banking institution which had done much to steer the country's economy through the ravages of war. Yet, though his was the most sober of professions, his thatch of fair hair and ruddy cheeks lent him a boyish appearance that was only belied by the good-humoured wrinkles around his eyes.

The third member of the company was Sir Edward Leithen, lawyer and MP and lately Solicitor General to His Majesty's Government. He had neither Lamancha's rangy build nor his other friend's huskiness, and yet there was about him an impression of great strength, as much inner as outer. He was paler than the others, partly because his occupation kept him indoors, but also as a result of a chlorine gas attack in the war that had left a faint yellow tinge to his complexion. His eyes, however, were bright, and testified to a deep power of thought that seemed to energise his sinews as much as his intellect. He was much admired by his colleagues and peers for that philosophical resilience of spirit that lent him the ability to turn mental insight into quick and decisive action.

Having dined well on freshly caught trout from the nearby river, the three friends were content to pursue their own individual forms of relaxation. Lamancha leafed through the latest edition of *The Field* while Leithen absorbed himself in a well-thumbed volume from the collected works of Sir Walter Scott, *The Talisman: Tales of the Crusaders*.

Palliser-Yeates was deftly constructing fishing flies from an assortment of materials laid out neatly in a sorting box on his knees. Pausing to stretch his neck, he took note of the title of Leithen's book and rolled his eyes.

'*The Talisman* again? Surely you've read that three or four times before.'

Leithen waved his friend's remark aside. 'When something is good, it deserves to be revisited. And I must say,' he added, tapping a finger on the page, 'Saladin's boldness in entering the Christian camp in disguise quite puts John Macnab's exploits in the shade.'

Lamancha set his empty glass aside and regarded his companions as he had once surveyed the ranks of his Australian cavalry brigade before launching them across the plains of Palestine. 'Do you suppose,' he suggested with an arched eyebrow, 'that we could do it all again?'

Palliser-Yeates came close to choking on his cigar. 'Hardly,' he scoffed. 'We were deucedly lucky to pull it off last time.'

'And to keep our anonymity,' added Leithen. 'We can be glad that only a few people know the true identities of the men concealed under the name of John Macnab.'

Only a year ago these three had set themselves a challenge: to overcome the stifling malaise that threatened to undo all the solid achievements of their distinguished lives. They defined their malady as a sort of disenchantment with the worldly success which seemed now to come to them too easily. It was Leithen who had characterised it as a sense that there was *nothing left remarkable beneath the visiting moon.*

The cure had been suggested unwittingly by their young friend Sir Archibald Roylance, who told them the tale of the near-legendary hunter Jim Tarras. Whenever he felt himself in a funk, Tarras would issue a challenge to local landowners, giving the exact date when he intended to bag a stag on their land, which he would then deliver up to them, for he was no thief. The aim was to create a contest of wits and daring between himself and the gamekeepers.

Lamancha had pounced on this as though a gauntlet had been flung at his feet, and had interrogated Archie about the estates surrounding Roylance's own lodge of Crask. Sweeping aside the cautious objections of Leithen and Palliser-Yeates, he insisted this was the tonic the three of them so desperately needed. By sheer force of his romantic vision he dragged his more sensible friends into his scheme of rejuvenation. Written challenges were mailed out to three landowners, each signed with the *nom de guerre* of John Macnab.

In the course of the adventure, sometimes by necessity, sometimes by accident, several other individuals were recruited to the cause of John Macnab, even as the fictional hero's exploits were blazed across the pages of the national press, displacing the latest strike and the tedious visit of an obscure foreign dignitary.

At the successful conclusion of the exploit, the three had agreed to reunite on the anniversary of John Macnab's triumph, though it had been decided to hold their celebration at an alternative venue to avoid the risk of their reappearance's being connected with those notorious events. Lamancha had arranged the lease of Rushforth Lodge, a neglected property in Denroy, some distance to the north of Machray.

The central feature of Denroy was Glen Shean, a serpentine cleft running east–west through a game-rich wilderness of forest, crag and moorland. The river Shean alternately rambled and rushed along the valley floor, fed at its upper end by small waterfalls cascading from the high ground amid outcrops of stone. To the north, the land grew ever more rough and challenging, seamed with burns and dotted with lochans. Mountain peaks loomed blue against the northerly horizon. So here they were, some way north of the original field of battle, at a neglected lodge on the southern edge of Denroy.

Lamancha refilled his glass. 'Don't tell me you've both settled back into your old routine without any sense of restlessness,' said Lamancha, refilling his glass. His easy smile took some of the sting from his scornful tone. 'Shouldn't we at least try to match the daring of the noble Saladin? Perhaps we should nip over to Balmoral and make off with the king's royal car, see how long it takes them to catch up with us.'

Leithen shook his head indulgently. 'Really, Charles, when you're in this sort of mood I'm half afraid you're going to turn into Dick Turpin.'

'We're certainly not going to bestir ourselves just for a piece of high jinks,' said Palliser-Yeates. 'We'd need to have some real purpose.'

'As the Crusaders in that book of yours looked to Jerusalem,' said Lamancha with a nod towards Leithen.

'But the Lionheart didn't pull it off, did he?' said Palliser-Yeates.

'No, he never did reach Jerusalem,' Leithen agreed, turning to Lamancha. 'You're one up on him there, Charles.'

They all knew that Lamancha had marched into Jerusalem with Allenby's army in 1917, capping a great victory over the Ottomans.

'That's true, though I can't say there's much peace to be found there even now,' said Lamancha ruefully.

'I don't imagine anyone will find their peace in the actual city,' said Leithen, 'but I think the vision that draws men on is that other place, the jewelled City of God.'

'The heavenly Jerusalem, eh?' said Palliser-Yeates gruffly. 'Well, I hope we can get a square meal there and a good claret.'

Noticing the glasses were empty, Lamancha refilled them all. 'A toast then,' he said, 'to whatever lies beyond the next hill.'

As they clinked glasses together, Leithen added, 'And to each man his own Jerusalem.'

They had barely taken a sip when they were interrupted by an urgent rapping at the front door. With Lamancha in the lead, the three men leapt from their seats and hurried down the hall. Charles flung open the door, revealing two figures on the doorstep.

The taller and stouter of the two was Lamancha's man Stokes. 'Sorry for the disturbance, Captain,' he rumbled. Having served under Lamancha in Palestine, he persisted in addressing him as an officer. 'I was setting out some snares when I found this chap here stumbling about in the shrubbery.'

Leaning on his arm was a wildly dishevelled stranger, soaking wet and covered in mud, his head hanging low from utter exhaustion.

'He mentioned Sir Edward by name,' Stokes continued. 'Said he'd come looking for him and it was desperately urgent.'

'Looking for me?' said Leithen in astonishment. 'What

on earth can he want?'

'Bring him inside,' ordered Lamancha, 'and we'll hear what he has to say for himself.'

At the sound of his voice, the stranger shook himself loose and staggered forward. With his next step he wavered and collapsed face down on the rug.

The three Macnabs gathered around the fallen man. His sodden clothing was shredded in many places, revealing an array of cuts and bruises beneath. Palliser-Yeates whistled softly through his teeth. 'Whoever this poor chap is, he's taken a real mauling.'

'Let's get him onto the sofa,' said Lamancha. 'Stokes, please fetch some water and towels.'

As Stokes departed, the Macnabs, who were accustomed to dealing with wounded men on the battlefield, gently lifted the stranger and laid him on his back on the sofa. When his face caught the light all three gaped in astonishment.

'Good God!' gasped Palliser-Yeates. 'It's Dick Hannay!'

When the water arrived Leithen began to wipe the grime from the stricken man's face. As he did so, Hannay's eyes flickered open. He seized Leithen's arm and stared at each of the three men in turn

'Ned, thank God I made it – and that you're all here!' he gasped. 'I need your help in what may be the most desperate endeavour of our lives'.

2

A MONARCH IN THE WILD

——

Richard Hannay's Narrative

I had not been back to Scotland since the affair of the Three Hostages. In the aftermath of those events I had needed time to recover from the injuries I had received at the hands of Dominick Medina, but also from the realisation that such individuals could exist – even thrive – in the very heart of our civilisation. The passage of time and the precious company of my wife Mary and Peter John, our five-year-old son, had done much to restore my spirits but a certain restlessness still tugged at me.

Much as I loved Fosse Manor, Mary's ancestral home in the Cotswolds, I had always felt drawn back to Scotland, the land of my birth. Those pristine forests and wild mountains were like a sanctuary where I could experience a sense of renewal. When a widowed cousin invited Mary and Peter John to join her and her own boy for a holiday in Bath, I might have gone with them, but I found myself craving activities more challenging than taking the waters and playing bridge of an evening in the hotel salon. After seeing off my wife and son on their travels, I embarked on a pilgrimage of my own.

I packed my gear and boarded a train for the north with the intention of heading up to Ullapool for some climbing at Assynt. After an overnight stay in Glasgow, I made an early start up the West Highland Railway line. I realised I was nearing Denroy, a region almost unrivalled for its rugged scenery and hunting prospects.

I recalled that my old friend Edward Leithen had told me he was meeting some friends here for a spot of hiking and fishing. Rushforth Lodge was the rendezvous point and he had given me a pretty good idea of its location. It suddenly struck me that this was exactly the sort of company I needed: men who, like me, were veterans of the war and relished the challenge of some physical activity.

It had always been my habit to value my instinct, and now it prompted me to follow this impulse. I left the train at a tiny rural stop where the portly station master gave me detailed instructions on how to reach Rushforth Lodge. Thanking him, I shouldered my pack and set out.

The path was well marked at the outset, a ribbon of hard-trodden ground descending in its early stages through swaths of bracken. Upland moor gave way presently to pitched stands of birch and hazel that fell away in terraced ranks towards the base of the glen. Eventually the path petered out, but by then I was within sight of the forestry road I had been told to look out for.

The angle of descent was steep, the intervening slope pocked with outcrops of boulders and thready watercourses, but by dint of careful going I arrived at the roadside and paused to reconnoitre. The road itself was an unpaved track riddled with potholes. On this side of the glen the ground was seamed with deep gouges, as if some primordial Titan had taken a blunt axe to wood and stone. With sharp bends to both east and west, it was impossible to see very far, but confident in my sense of direction I squared my shoulders and set off westward.

I could not help but reflect that the last time I was in this country, I was being hunted by the brilliant Dominick Medina, and my left hand still bore a scar where his bullet had struck me. Enemy that he was, I could yet admire his genius, his energy, his singleness of purpose. If those gifts had been turned to good instead of twisted to brutish and avaricious ends, what monuments might that man have raised up?

As rogue beasts such men were dangerous enough, but what made them truly terrible was that they found the means to form, out of local gangs, national and international networks of intrigue and violence. Incapable as they were of anything as decent as friendship or fellow feeling, what bound them together was a shared contempt for the ordinary man, who was simply there to be manipulated and enslaved. Medina and his crew had no qualms about making hostages of innocent children to clear the path for their schemes, such were the devilish depths to which they sank.

In the end, their actions had not even the dignity of logic. When his organisation was dismantled, Medina had the option of continuing to live as a prominent and wealthy figure. Instead he chose to hunt me through these very hills. His aim was not to remove an obstacle from his path but only to inflict bloody vengeance upon one who had already been instrumental in his downfall. This spiteful course led him to his own death, even though at the end I did my best to save him.

Shaking off these sombre thoughts, I returned my attention to the refreshing beauty of my surroundings.

Off to my right, a full-born river raced downward over shelves of rock. On the opposite bank lay a lush green sward studded with wild flowers against a backdrop of boulders and willow trees. At a turn in the road I paused to take a sip from my water bottle. When I lowered my head I glimpsed something that made my heart leap with pleasure.

No more than thirty yards from me stood a lordly stag, the most magnificent I had ever beheld. Head erect, ears alert, he was surveying his realm with the imperious air of a true monarch. He was perhaps in his fifth year, sleek and well muscled, with a fine head of ten points.

Until you have stumbled upon them in the wild, you cannot imagine how such a large animal can be rendered invisible by its dun-coloured hide. It is almost an exact match for the muted and mottled shades of its surroundings. My unsuspecting eye had passed carelessly over him, and only a slight movement of his magnificent antlers had put me on alert.

I smiled across at him and raised my hand in salute. He seemed to lift his head in a dignified acknowledgement. All at once I found myself laughing. At some spiritual level this encounter had thoroughly dispelled my recent grim reflections.

Here was a reminder that, in the face of the wanton caprices of man, Nature herself is not chaotic. If anything, she is more orderly than even the highest civilisation, with the round of the seasons, the migrations of birds and fish, the regularity of the harvest. The honest rhythms of Nature are the opposite of chaos and will always triumph over it, and so will men if they hold fast to the image that is stamped upon their souls.

All at once something seemed to startle the stag. He tossed his head, sniffed the air and bolted off in a flurry of pounding hooves. I glanced around and saw a man emerge out of a fold in the ground some distance behind and below me, working his way towards me up the glen.

Seen from a distance, the stranger appeared to be in his sixties, hale and fit for his age. He was not a local man, for there was something continental in the cut of his brown woollen walking suit and the style of his hunting cap. He had on stout leather boots and carried an alpenstock, gripping it firmly in his right hand while keeping his left in his coat pocket.

Something flickered at the back of my mind but I could not put my finger on what was familiar about the stranger. Meanwhile he continued to approach. He was clearly in a state of suppressed agitation for he kept darting glances about him, as if he were on the lookout for someone.

When he spotted me he stopped short, squinting curiously. I walked towards him and called, 'Hello! Can I be of any assistance?'

'Do you know these parts well?' he asked. His tone conveyed a mixture of anxiety and hope.

'I'm just visiting,' I told him. 'I'm on my way to join some friends.'

'I, also, am with friends,' said the stranger, 'but we seem to have lost one another. I have been looking for them without success.'

'Perhaps I can help you find them, Mr . . . ?'

He gave a hesitant smile. 'Hesselmann, Konrad Hesselmann. I am a banker here on holiday from Geneva.

And you?'

'Hannay,' I replied, 'Richard Hannay. I'm also on holiday. When did you last see your friends?'

'Last night before we all retired to bed.'

'Did they mention any plans to be off early?'

He shook his head. 'When my aide and I woke this morning they had simply disappeared.'

'They didn't leave a note or anything.'

'Again, no. I am concerned on their behalf. To be honest, I am unsure if I can find my own way back.'

'Perhaps I can guide you and help you search?' I offered.

'That is very kind of you, Mr Hannay. Perhaps we should head back towards the cottage where we were staying?' He pointed a thumb back over his shoulder. 'I do not think they would have strayed any further than this.'

As we set off I made a closer assessment of my new acquaintance. His craggy face was dominated by pale, somewhat haggard eyes. His high-bridged nose and full white beard gave him an air of distinction and the way he carried himself suggested a retired military man.

Suddenly – with a flash of recognition – I was carried back in my mind to a wintry railway platform on the edge of a small German town in 1915. I was masquerading as Cornelius Brandt, a South African engineer so consumed with hatred of the British that he was willing to offer his services to their Prussian enemies.

There, in the midst of a group of elderly officers, I was introduced to a man a little below average height, muffled in a thick coat with a fur collar. He wore a silver helmet with an eagle atop it, and kept his left hand resting on his sword.

Beneath the helmet was a face the colour of grey paper from which shone sombre, restless eyes with dark pouches below them. It was the face of one who slept little and whose thoughts rode him like a nightmare.

In the man before me the sharply upturned military moustache had melted into a soft snow-white beard, and his military bearing now spoke less of arrogance than of an old man's pride. Yet there was no doubt in my mind that this was the very man who had once been my sworn enemy.

Wilhelm II, the ex-Kaiser of Germany.

3

THE HUNGRY RIVER

——

How the ex-ruler of Germany came to be wandering among the peaks and glens of Denroy was a mystery of colossal proportions.

As the perceived instigator of the Great War, Wilhelm was the most hated man in Europe, perhaps in the world. To avoid being brought to trial for the atrocities committed in his name, he had been forced into permanent exile in Holland, forbidden to venture more than twenty-five miles from his estate at Doorn. It was as much as his life was worth to leave that refuge. Yet here he was – and by his own account he had not come alone.

A covert side-glance at my companion reassured me that he had not recognised me in turn – and why should he? At the time of our encounter, I was merely one more cog in a complex military machine. The Kaiser of Germany had more weighty matters on his mind than the face of a chance acquaintance at a period when the outcome of the war still hung in the balance.

At the time he had not struck me as a madman or a barbaric despot, as he was so often depicted. On the contrary, he seemed to me a man a shade too ordinary for his exalted position, who lacked the powers of intellect or wisdom needed to steer his country on a sane course. Instead, through his own arrogance and ambition, he had uncaged a savage beast upon the world and he feared its rampage as much as anyone. My reflection then had been that I would not swap places with him for all the blessings of Heaven.

Whatever had brought him to Scotland, it was clearly a secret venture unsanctioned by conventional channels of diplomacy. I sensed a game being played for high stakes, and against all odds fate had placed me in a unique position to find out what it was.

I would have to tread carefully to avoid putting the Kaiser on his guard. I schooled my face to an easy smile and resumed our conversation. 'So, Herr Hesselmann, are you in Scotland on business or to do a spot of hunting and fishing?'

'For pleasure and relaxation, of course.' He sounded quite genuine. 'Shooting would be a pleasure, though it is years since I held a rifle. Now, however, I am hunting for those missing colleagues of mine. You say you have seen no one?'

'Not a soul,' I affirmed.

I noted that his English was quite perfect and barely accented. That was only to be expected, I supposed, given that his mother was an English princess, the daughter of Queen Victoria, and the young Wilhelm had been a frequent visitor to his grandmother's court.

I decided to risk probing further. 'Have you been long in Denroy?'

'We arrived yesterday evening. We dined at eight and after drinks retired to bed. I confess I overslept this morning, as did my aide. I expect your Scottish air is responsible. When we rose we found the two who had accompanied us had disappeared, taking their car with them.'

'Your missing friends are Swiss also?'

He blinked twice before replying. 'They are indeed countrymen of mine. I sent my aide to the east to look for them while I explored to the west. Perhaps by the time we find our way back to the cottage they will have returned.'

To our left the glen dropped steeply to where the Shean river tumbled impetuously over a string-course of boulders. On the other side a jagged scar ran down the sheer hillside as though it had been defaced by a blunt and angry dagger. Down this defile a shimmering waterfall dashed headlong from the heights, racing for the torrent below like a frenzy of crazed hares.

'I do enjoy your Scottish countryside,' said my companion. Then he added in the tone of a guilty confession, 'But what I am most looking forward to are some good Scottish scones. I had a Scottish housekeeper once who used to bake them fresh for me with jam and cream.'

Suddenly there was a disturbance among the tree-clad slopes ahead. Glancing upward, I saw a flock of startled rooks explode into the air just before three men hove into view on the road from the east.

The Kaiser gave a reflexive start at the sight then commanded himself. I realised how wary he must be of being recognised, but the great majority of people only knew him from old photographs in the newspapers. In those pictures his hair was darker, his moustache stiff and twisted upward, and he was always in a uniform bedecked with medals. No one who had not met him could possibly identify this modestly attired businessman with the imperious Prussian of old.

As the newcomers drew nearer, I saw they were dressed like huntsmen and all carried rifles. The foremost wore a patch over his right eye and a bitter scowl twisted the mouth beneath his bristling black moustache. At his heels came a large, flat-faced man with grizzled brown hair and a close-cropped beard beside whom walked a lad with a tangle of brown curls. He resembled the man at his side so closely, they were undoubtedly father and son.

Something in their purposeful stride sent a tingle of alarm down my spine. I stopped and placed my hand gently on the Kaiser's arm to restrain him. He turned on me with an affronted glare and snorted peevishly. I realised he was not accustomed to anyone's laying hands on him and immediately released my grip.

'Those aren't your friends?' I enquired.

'Indeed not,' he replied. 'I have never seen these men before.'

The leader of the strangers unslung the rifle from his shoulder and levelled it at us. 'Gentlemen, you are trespassing on private land.'

'As far as I am aware, this is no one's property,' I retorted.

The one-eyed man ignored my objection. 'I must ask you to identify yourselves.'

'My name is Richard Hannay,' I told him. My sense of danger was growing, but I could see no alternative to holding our ground.

'And I am Herr Hesselmann,' the Kaiser informed him stiffly.

The glances passing between the three men told me they recognised the name.

'And you are together?' One Eye pressed.

'Mr Hannay was kind enough to alter direction,' said Wilhelm, 'so that he might help me find my way.'

'That won't be necessary now.' The lead huntsman shooed me off with a wave of his rifle. 'You can carry on to wherever you were going, Mr Hannay. We'll escort *Herr Hesselmann* to his destination.'

The Kaiser took a step back, sensing that something was amiss. He drew himself up with dignity and addressed the newcomers haughtily. 'I do not believe that will be necessary. Your assistance is not required.'

'I must insist.' One Eye signalled his associates and they advanced on us with their guns at the ready. It was clear to me now that they knew exactly who Wilhelm was and that they intended him no good.

Snatching the alpenstock from the Kaiser's fingers, I yelled, 'Run!'

Perhaps for the first time in his life the former emperor proved as quick to obey an order as he was to give one and bounded off up the westward road.

One Eye grabbed the young man by the shoulder and propelled him forward. 'After him!'

The youth raced off in pursuit while the other two closed with me. With a whirl of the alpenstock I dashed the gun from the leader's hands. As he recoiled with a curse, I threw my shoulder into him and sent him crashing into a nest of bracken.

The man with the grizzled hair turned his rifle on me, but I rammed the alpenstock into his midriff. With a pained grunt he staggered backward against a tree and went down.

I took off after the Kaiser, but before I could get more than a few yards, a shot rang out and a bullet whined over my head. I dived instinctively to the ground, and the moment I rolled onto my back Greybeard was on me again.

He slung the rifle over his shoulder and seized the alpenstock with both hands. I pulled him down and we rolled back and forth, wrestling for the weapon. One Eye came up on my right and swung the butt of his gun at me like a club. I tried to dodge the blow but he caught me a glancing crack on the cheek.

My head was ringing as I scrambled desperately away, leaving Greybeard with the alpenstock. My attackers bore down on me and hauled me to my feet. I clipped One Eye on the chin with my elbow, but they took a firm grip and hustled me roughly towards the precipitous embankment overlooking the river. Thirty feet below the water churned and roared like a hungry beast. Even as I dug my heels in and tried to resist, my opponents gave me a violent shove that pitched me over the edge.

My hands clutched for a hold but all they met was empty air as I tumbled uncontrollably down the drastic drop, bashing off boulders and saplings without an instant's pause to even think of the damage I was taking. One moment I was sliding face first through the bracken, the next my heels were whipping over my head, my body tossed about like a toy. The breath was knocked clear out of my lungs and I saw the whirling landscape pivot about me in a blur of crimson mist.

I caught only a flashing glimpse of the river rushing up to meet me as my left leg rammed through a bush, twisting me about so that my crown was aimed directly at the bottom. I hit the water like a cannonball going through a wall, plunging straight down until I scraped grazingly along the gritty bottom.

Even as I thrashed upward, fighting my way to the light, the current snatched me away in an angry rush, as though punishing me for my intrusion. Battered as I was by the fall, I had not the strength to resist the charge of the water and the icy chill was soaking through my clothes.

After what felt like the struggle of a lifetime, my head broke the surface and I sucked in a hungry gulp of air. Before I could take in anything else I was flung over a vertical waterfall and shot down with limbs flailing. The pool below smacked me hard, and as I went down a voracious undercurrent snatched at my legs, yanking me into the airless dark.

As soon as my feet touched the bottom, I thrust myself upward and broke out into the air again. Arms and legs threshing, I kept myself from being dragged down once more, but could not prevent the savage current from carrying me off like a runaway carriage. Dazed and weakened by the fall, staying afloat was all I could manage until my vision cleared and I could think straight again.

I don't know how far I was swept along before a bend in the river brought me momentarily within reach of the rocky shore. In one swift lunge I caught hold of a dangling tree root with one hand and hung on with all the determination of a drowning man. My strength felt as nothing compared to the violence of the current, but

I hauled myself closer to my lifeline until I could grasp it in both hands and drag myself inch by inch out of the clutches of the river.

The stony bank was so slimy with wet moss, I could barely gain any purchase, but I finally worked my way clear of the water and crawled to a patch of soggy ground at the foot of a wizened beech. I think I must have passed out for a while, because the next thing I remember was seeing the sun sinking to the west, which at least gave me some sense of direction.

Leaning against the tree for support, I painstakingly manoeuvred my way up onto my feet and forced my legs to stay firm. My clothes were soaked, scuffed and torn and my body felt the same way. There was a sharp chill in the air that caused the bruises and cuts I had collected to ache and sting like the very devil. I thanked the Lord that nothing was broken, for I was a long way from the nearest help.

I made a laborious climb to higher ground, using branches and tussocks to pull myself up the steep incline like an ill-equipped mountaineer. At last I had a clear view of the landscape, an untamed expanse of rolling hills and unchecked forest. I scanned in every direction until I caught sight of that curious double peak that is unique to Ben Truach.

Now that I had my bearings, I set out, stumbling and staggering, in the direction of Rushforth Lodge. I was in desperate need of help, not for myself, but for that hapless gentleman who had fallen into the clutches of men who gave every indication of a ruthless intent.

4

THE KNIGHTS ADVANCE

_____

After providing the welcome comforts of water, soap and towels, as well as a plate of cold beef sandwiches and a fresh bottle of whisky, the ever discreet Stokes absented himself while I related the day's extraordinary events to my three friends.

I told the tale as briefly as I could, focusing chiefly on the Kaiser's abduction. They listened in an attentive silence broken only by some muttered exclamations of surprise. As I concluded my report Lamancha let out a low whistle.

Palliser-Yeates shook his head incredulously. 'If I heard a yarn like that from anyone but you, Dick, I'd write it off as pure bosh.'

'So you see,' by now my voice was weak and hoarse, 'we must track down those men and rescue the Kaiser.'

Now that I had found refuge and passed on the vital information, I felt sheer exhaustion overwhelm me. Leithen had to steady me as I fought to keep my eyes open.

'Look, Dick,' he said, 'it's pitch black out and you're completely done in. Let's get you off to bed and I promise we'll pick up the trail in the morning.'

I nodded numbly and succumbed to my overpowering fatigue. I was dimly aware of friendly hands transporting me to one of the bedrooms before a dreamless dark swallowed me up.

When I awoke in the morning and creaked out of bed, I discovered that Stokes had boiled a huge kettle of water and filled a tin bathtub for me. Pressing as my business was, I couldn't help basking for several minutes while the soapy warmth soothed my aching muscles and bruises. Once I had towelled off, I donned a set of Lamancha's spare clothing which had been laid out for me. Thoroughly refreshed, I made my way to the kitchen, drawn on by the ambrosial scents of best bacon and freshly laid eggs.

All four of us gathered round the table and Leithen took charge of the impromptu conference while we set about the enormous breakfast Stokes had conjured up.

'I've been giving this a lot of thought,' he said, 'and I'm sure your hunch is right, Dick: Wilhelm would not be risking his neck just for the sake of a holiday. He's here for some deeper purpose.'

'Which seems to have backfired on him,' Palliser-Yeates commented as he helped himself to a few extra rashers of bacon.

'It's among the conditions of the Versailles treaty that he should be tried for his crimes,' said Lamancha. 'He only dodged that by hiding out in Holland.'

I took a bite of toast and washed it down with a swallow of tea. 'I recall that right after the war the newspapers were full of demands to *Hang the Kaiser!*' I quoted a popular headline of the time. 'The government eventually decided to let it drop, rather than stir up more trouble in Germany.'

'Well, he's in somebody's hands now,' Lamancha reminded us all. 'So who the deuce are they?'

'From your description of the one-eyed man,' Leithen

told me, 'I'd say that's Hamish Mackinnon, Kildennan's head gamekeeper.'

Lamancha leaned forward sharply. 'You mean Lord Duncan Kildennan?'

'That's the chap,' Leithen confirmed. 'His estate is up north on the other side of Glen Shean. I've met him a few times socially, at hunt balls, testimonial dinners and suchlike.'

'I'm not acquainted with him,' said Palliser-Yeates. 'What sort of a chap is he?'

'I saw him in action in London,' said Lamancha, 'holding raucous meetings and making firebrand speeches. Before he retired up here to his ancestral estate, he was one of the founders of the National Banner movement along with the likes of General Blakely and Lord Kelburn.'

'I've heard of that lot,' I put in. 'Aren't they admirers of Signor Mussolini?'

'That's right,' said Lamancha. 'They think our country could do with a dose of the same medicine that he's dishing out.'

'It might be best to see how that turns out in Italy before we try swallowing any of it here,' said Leithen quietly.

'They've certainly got the frights up about Bolshevism,' said Palliser-Yeates, 'and I can't say I blame them for that overmuch.'

'So if it is Kildennan's men who seized the Kaiser,' I wondered, 'what exactly do they plan to do with him?'

Leithen's brow furrowed in foreboding. 'I've been running through all I know about Kildennan, and one terrible fact stands out in my mind: he lost two sons in the war.'

There was a moment of grim silence as we all pondered this.

'In that case, I don't think his intentions towards our old foe can possibly be friendly,' said Lamancha.

'No,' I agreed. 'Those men of his definitely had a ruthless purpose in mind. I have an awful notion that he plans to dispense the justice many thought should have been carried out years ago. Can he really be so careless of the consequences?'

'I've heard it said that the grief has been eating away inside him for years now,' said Leithen, 'to the point where he no longer has the patience for politics as usual or for the slow workings of the law.'

'It's pretty clear,' I concluded, 'that Kildennan is planning his own private hanging.'

'Then we must contact the proper authorities at once,' Palliser-Yeates advised.

'No, that's quite impossible,' I objected.

Palliser-Yeates treated me to a puzzled frown but Leithen came to my support. 'Dick's quite right. This is a man half the country would cheerfully see swing from the gallows.'

'If word of this should leak out, the consequences could be disastrous,' Lamancha agreed. 'No, this is a job for us alone and we can't involve anyone else.' I couldn't help but detect a certain relish in his tone at the prospect.

'Regardless of the legal situation,' I said, 'if the Kaiser should simply be murdered here on British soil, there would be an international uproar. Germany might explode. For all we know it could bring on another war.'

Palliser-Yeates indicated his displeasure with a loud

clearing of his throat. 'I suppose you're right, but it certainly puts us on the spot.'

'What beats me,' said Lamancha, 'is this: if he's here in secret, how on earth did Kildennan get wind of it?'

'There are others involved,' I reminded him. 'Wilhelm told me as much. Somebody must have let word slip in the wrong quarter.'

Lamancha turned his lively gaze on me. 'So what's the plan?'

'We need to find Wilhelm before Kildennan carries out whatever he's planning and get him safely out of the country,' I said.

'How do we go about it then?' Lamancha rubbed his chin as he assessed the options. 'I don't think making a frontal assault on Kildennan's castle is likely to improve the situation.'

'No, we don't want to force his hand,' I agreed. 'If we go charging in, he may just take his revenge right away with a bullet.'

'We need to take it softly,' said Leithen. 'I suggest Dick and I motor up to Kildennan's place as though we were making a social call. I know him well enough to make that wash.'

'And what about the rest of us?' asked Palliser-Yeates.

'From what Wilhelm said, he has friends wandering around out there, probably just as lost as he was,' I recalled. 'You and Charles should track those fellows down. They may have the answers to a lot of our questions.'

'A manhunt, eh?' said Lamancha eagerly. 'It will be interesting to be on the other side of one this time.'

'Yes, that should prove a worthy challenge for the daring John Macnab,' I commented wrily.

There was a moment of silence, then Leithen gave a slow smile.

'So you guessed it.'

'I suspected for some time, but finding all of you here on the very anniversary of Macnab's exploits – well, you don't have to be Sherlock Holmes to figure it out.'

As I took a last swallow of tea, I looked round at the three of them and reflected that in such a situation a man could not have better company or better allies. 'So does this mean that I'm now an honorary Macnab?'

'Dick,' said Lamancha, saluting me with his teacup, 'I'm pretty sure you've been a Macnab all along.'

As we loaded up Leithen's Ford car, Lamancha fed Stokes a line about a pheasant shoot. Stokes was no fool and was clearly aware that something was up, but in years of soldiering he had learned that sometimes an officer was compelled to play things close to his chest. He asked no questions of his captain but merely assured him that he was ready to be called upon should the need arise.

As we drove off Lamancha glanced back at his man. 'It feels low not to trust Stokes with the truth, but the fewer people we drag into this business the better.'

I was up front with Leithen, who was driving carefully over a rough track that was capable of playing merry hell with the suspension of any vehicle that did not treat it with due deference.

'I expect Kildennan is in the same position,' I said. 'The fewer lips there are to blab his plans, the safer for him.'

'With any luck then,' growled Palliser-Yeates, 'the odds may be just about even.'

'If you two can catch up to Wilhelm's German friends,' said Leithen, 'that might tip the balance in our favour.'

Lamancha leaned a nonchalant elbow on the open rear window and drew out a thin cigar. He struck a match and the flame reflected in his eyes. 'The game's afoot then. Here we are, a band of white knights riding to the rescue of the black king.'

After a few miles we pulled up to let Lamancha and Palliser-Yeates jump out with their rifles. I pointed the way up to the spot where I had encountered the Kaiser and his pursuers.

'I don't know that I'm entirely happy to be splitting our forces like this,' Palliser-Yeates complained.

'John has a point,' Lamancha agreed. 'We should decide on a rendezvous point where we can catch up with you.'

'Well, if we manage to prise our man away from Kildennan,' said Leithen, 'our best bet would be to make for the coast.'

Lamancha took a thoughtful draw on his cigar. 'Headed west then, eh? Do you know that old ruin Castle Crachan?'

'I think so,' I said. 'It's on the shore of Loch Dhuie.'

'That's it,' said Lamancha. 'You can hole up there out of sight until you see a chance to get clear or until we come to join you.'

With that our two friends waved us a farewell and began their ascent.

Leithen started us back on our way, bumping and jerking over the uneven ground.

We crossed a stone bridge over the lower reaches of the Shean river and joined a more satisfactory road coming in from the west. It carried us north through a cluster of bare hills and into a dense forest that might have hidden a small army in the olden days of the clan wars.

When we emerged from the woodland the road opened out into a broad oak-lined avenue leading up to a russet castle with a pair of crenellated turrets and a frowning battlement. As we pulled up by the massive front door we spotted a lean man in a black bonnet keeping watch from the taller of the two towers. The barrel of his gun was visible leaning against the parapet, but for now it was only his eyes that were taking aim at us.

As we climbed out and ambled innocently up to the great house, I couldn't help glancing back to where our rifles were locked in the boot of the car. We had decided beforehand to appear as casual and non-threatening as possible so as not to provoke Kildennan into any precipitate action, but doing so rendered us extremely vulnerable.

We climbed five or six well-worn steps to the great wooden door, which was guarded on each side by a granite mastiff resting on its haunches with its stony teeth bared. 'So, Ned,' I said, in a voice loud enough for the man watching us to overhear, 'I hope this place is worth the drive. If you ask me, all these old castles look alike.'

With that I gave the bell pull a good yank.

'Now we'll see what we're up against,' said Leithen under his breath as the bell jangled tinnily inside.

I braced myself to behold the face of our enemy.

5

TEA WITH THE RED QUEEN

———

We waited a full minute and it became clear that no one was in any hurry to let us in. Eventually the great door creaked open a few meagre inches and the round face of a pale little housemaid blinked out at us.

'Gentlemen?' she enquired in a small, piping voice. She appeared reluctant to offer us more than that one word.

'Is Lord Kildennan at home?' Leithen responded in a kindly tone.

The girl hesitated and bit her lip, then looked back over her shoulder to where a rather more formidable figure was advancing down the shadowy hallway.

She was a tall young woman in a tweed jacket and skirt and a pair of riding boots. Her long auburn hair, tied with a black ribbon, caught a glint of the sun as she dismissed the maid and faced us squarely in the doorway. Her strong, handsome features suggested the beauty of the wild rose rather than that of the garden. Right now her thorns were only too apparent.

'Might I ask who is calling?' Her request carried the force of a challenge.

'I am Sir Edward Leithen, and this is my friend . . .'

'Richard Hannay.' I gave a small bow that made no impression.

'Is my father expecting you?' she demanded with brusque formality.

Though she looked to be no older than her late twenties,

I had the impression that her experience of life had lent her a gravity beyond her years.

'Not as such,' Leithen confessed. 'However, when I spoke to him recently, I believe it was a reception at Chattington Hall . . .'

'Lord Kildennan has not been down in London for some time,' the young woman interrupted.

'I expect it was last year. The point is that he did say I should come by and have a look at the place any time I was in the area.'

'I see. That was very hospitable of him.'

'Well, at the moment I am holidaying in Denroy.'

'And I am lodging with Sir Edward for a couple of days,' I added. 'He suggested a jaunt to Castle Kildennan might be just the thing to shake off the rust of an indolent summer.'

'Surely Lord Kildennan has spoken of me,' Leithen suggested.

'He has not,' the young woman returned. 'Nor of you, Mr Hannay.' Her sharp, hazel eyes narrowed as she assessed my bruised face. 'You appear to have taken a tumble.'

'I did have a bit of a mishap yesterday, but nothing I can't recover from.'

'Well, I suppose you had better come inside,' she conceded, waving us onward.

As we walked past her I saw her raise her hand to give a barely perceptible signal to the man on watch above before following us inside and closing the door.

'I'm Christina Kildennan,' she finally introduced herself.

'The lady of the house?' Leithen queried.

'Since my mother passed away, yes. I hope that I can adequately entertain you in my father's absence.'

To the right of the spacious entrance hall were two doors, while on the other side was another door and an open archway from which wafted odours suggestive of a kitchen somewhere beyond. Facing us, and leading to the upper floors, was a wide stone staircase, down which bounded an enormous, shaggy wolfhound. He eyed us with even less good humour than his mistress as he took up station at her side. Christina allowed herself a thin smile as she stroked the beast's great head.

'Don't mind Fearghal – he's been trained never to eat visitors.'

'That's very reassuring,' I said, though I suspected that one word of command from his mistress could render him considerably less placid. The dog watched us warily while we admired the array of basket-hilted swords, targes, banners and dirks that decorated the walls, symbols of a long martial tradition.

'Has his lordship gone away on business?' Leithen asked.

'He's not gone far,' Christina replied cautiously. 'He's over at the cattle pen inspecting some stock we recently purchased at market.'

I scrutinised the portrait of a bearded chieftain with a white cockade in his bonnet, wondering how much of a resemblance he bore to the absent laird. 'There's an impressive history here,' I remarked.

'The Kildennans rose in the '45,' she informed us, 'and paid a heavy price for it. Much of what you see here was hidden away for years while Cumberland and King George were taking their revenge.'

She took a step towards the archway and called out to the timid maid, who was, I assumed, lurking back there out of sight.

'Margaret! Bring us up a pot of tea and some of that shortbread.'

'There's really no need,' Leithen demurred as she led us through one of the right-hand doors,

The room beyond had tall windows overlooking a rose garden and a second door leading to an adjoining room. To our left, above the fireplace, hung an age-darkened oil painting depicting rival bands of clansmen setting about each other with bloodied swords. Facing the hearth was a leather-upholstered sofa, with a table of polished oak in front of it and two matching chairs at either end. On our right were two more chairs flanking a Welsh dresser.

'Hospitality does have its rules,' said Christina, ushering us towards the seats. 'Let it never be said that Castle Kildennan does not know how to treat a guest. Expected or otherwise,' she added pointedly.

While Leithen and I settled ourselves into our chairs, Christina leaned an elbow on the mantelpiece beside a silver clock whose ticking sounded unnaturally loud to me. I was painfully aware that every second might be bringing the ex-Kaiser closer to his end.

'I gather you don't get many visitors out here,' I offered, hoping to glean some notion of the prisoner's whereabouts.

'Not many that are welcome,' returned the lady of the house. 'I suppose with the history of this place, the very bricks themselves are soaked through with suspicion. But you gentlemen, of course, are simply here on holiday and understandably curious about my father's lodging.'

'It certainly looks capable of holding off intruders,' Leithen observed.

'These walls have seen their share of that,' Christina agreed. 'Not that there's any call for such defensiveness in these peaceful times. There's no one needing to be seen off forcefully these days but political candidates and persistent evangelists.'

'Might we have a tour of the house?' I wondered. 'If it's not inconvenient.'

'You must have your tea first,' our hostess insisted as the maid bustled in with a heavily laden tray.

The girl laid out the cups, milk, sugar and teapot and set a plate of shortbread in the middle of the table while her mistress left her station at the fireplace to slowly circumnavigate the room with the shaggy hound at her heels. When the maid had left, Christina bent to pour the tea then stood over us as we drank, like a guard overseeing a pair of prisoners.

'You know, I hate to put you out like this,' said Leithen. 'Perhaps you could direct us to where we can find Lord Kildennan and then we'll be out of your hair.'

While we sampled the shortbread, Christina took up position behind one of the empty chairs with her arms crossed across its back.

'No, you're no trouble to me, I assure you. Besides, by now my father will be wandering all over the estate. He likes to pay personal attention to everything that's going on. Far better that you wait for him here. I'm sure he won't be more than an hour, two at the most.'

I helped myself to a second finger of shortbread and sat back in my chair in a show of contentment. 'Well, you certainly serve up a fine tea, so waiting is no hardship.'

'If you'll excuse me a few moments, gentlemen,' Christina moved towards the door, 'I have one or two minor domestic matters to attend to. I'll not be long.'

Leithen took a swallow of tea. 'Of course. We'll be right here.'

As soon as the door closed behind our hostess and her imposing hound, I jumped up and addressed Leithen.

'Do you think they're keeping him in one of the rooms in the castle?'

Leithen stood and shook his head emphatically. 'Too many servants to pick up on what's happening, and, of course, the danger of visitors. No, he'll be somewhere more isolated.'

'And the girl? Is she in on it?'

'Absolutely. She's been left here to hold the fort and keep intruders like us from poking around.'

Signalling my friend to keep silence, I padded over to the door and opened it a crack. Through the gap I saw Christina Kildennan issuing instructions in a hushed voice to a young man I recognised as being the one who had given chase to the ex-Kaiser yesterday.

As they disappeared through an archway I ducked back into the room and briefly reported what I had seen to Leithen.

'Do you think she's sending him with a message to Kildennan?' he speculated.

'That seems likely.' I pointed to the small door in the

corner by the outer wall. 'If we can sneak out back, maybe we can see where he's going.'

That door led to a small passage that took us through a storeroom to a back exit. We crept swiftly across the rear courtyard and took shelter behind a corner of the stables. Without speaking a word, I drew Leithen's attention to a path leading up into the hills that crowded up on each other behind the castle. There was that same young man tramping up through the trees towards some unseen destination.

We set off after him swiftly, using all the stealth we had acquired from years of stalking deer without alerting them to our presence. This was much easier as there was plenty of cover and he never once glanced back. I had a feeling that his father would have chided him if he had observed his careless demeanour.

The house disappeared behind us, hidden by a turn in the hills, and the path wound over increasingly difficult ground. The trees grew thicker, but still we kept our quarry in sight. Occasionally he stopped to get his bearings and we crouched low in the shadows to evade any wandering of his eye.

Finally, after a trek of two miles or so, he reached the top of a ridge and disappeared over the far side. We hurried to the crest then slid down to where the thick heather would conceal us from view. In the glen below we saw the ruins of a long abandoned village. Many of the cottages were no more than flat patterns of broken stone or piles of rubble littering the ground. A few were relatively intact, while one or two appeared to have undergone some degree of restoration.

Two men with rifles were seated on the stump of a wall. One was a lanky, cadaverous individual, the other I recognised from the previous day as the father of the young messenger. At the sight of his son he stood and waved a greeting as the youth hurried down to join them.

'This is the place,' I muttered to Leithen as we wriggled further under cover. 'They must be holding Wilhelm in one of those buildings.'

'Do you think we have a chance of sneaking down there and freeing him,' Leithen wondered, 'unarmed as we are?'

'We've no time to go back for our guns or fetch the others,' I said.

Even as I pondered our options, three sharp hoots suddenly pierced the air. The two guards were instantly on alert. Waving the youngster aside, they started up the slope towards us, rifles raised to fire.

I whipped about to see where the warning cry had come from. There was Christina Kildennan standing tall on the crest. A rifle rested in the crook of her arm and such was her confidence in her own abilities, she did not even feel the need to point it at us. At her side the great hound was poised and ready to spring at his mistress's command.

'Gentlemen,' she said without mirth, 'I thought I told you to bide where you were.'

6

THE JUDGEMENT TREE

The guards had spotted us and rushed up the slope with their weapons at the ready. My first impulse was to bolt before they got any closer, dashing and dodging as best we could, but I saw Leithen give the slightest shake of his head.

'If we cut and run it will force their hand,' he warned me in a murmur. 'Wilhelm would be dead before we could raise the alarm anywhere.'

I knew he was right. Besides, not only did Christina Kildennan's hound look more than capable of chasing us down, I had a shrewd intuition that his mistress would turn out to be a crack shot. The wisest course, now that we had been flushed out, was to give ourselves up and look for an opportunity to turn the tables.

We stood up to face Christina as she descended towards us with the dog padding a few feet ahead. Leithen and I had been rather pleased with ourselves for shadowing our quarry undetected, but this young woman's tracking skills had put us to shame. Yet rather than showing any sense of pride at having cornered us, she seemed irked at being put to the trouble.

'If you had done as I told you, we would not be in this situation,' she informed us sternly. 'You have only yourselves to blame for whatever comes next.'

Fearghal uttered a displeased growl that served to reinforce his mistress's rebuke.

'Did you really expect us to sit and drink tea, knowing what we know?' I said.

'I thought you might have that much sense,' she answered. 'And the shortbread is worth savouring. Do you imagine that by blundering into this business you are doing anything but making matters worse?'

Worse for whom? I wondered. For her father and herself who now had to deal with witnesses to their kidnapping? For their prisoner? Or for ourselves?

When the guards reached us we were escorted down into the centre of the abandoned village, which was dominated by a huge, gnarled oak, its bark pitted and scarred like the face of a mountain. Beyond the tree was a circle of crumbling stones surrounding a long disused well.

While the tall, pale-faced man kept an eye on us, the father and son conferred in low voices. Christina walked over to one of the restored cottages and called to those inside. The one-eyed Mackinnon came out first, followed by a man who could only be the laird, Duncan Kildennan.

He did indeed bear some resemblance to the long dead chieftain whose portrait I had noted back at the castle. He was a good six feet tall with thick brown hair worn longer than was common. This and his broad beard were flecked with grey and a pair of bushy brows hung over his fiery eyes.

Mackinnon murmured a word in his chief's ear then fell into step behind him.

'It's as well, Kirsty, that I left you on guard at home,' Kildennan told his daughter in a rich baritone. 'We can't have these fine gentlemen wandering about, getting themselves into trouble.'

'I knew them for what they were the moment they came to the door,' Christina reported. She gave her father a brief account of our visit to Castle Kildennan and her pursuit of us through the hills.

The laird turned to us and nodded appraisingly.

'Sir Edward, I had not expected to encounter you in this forsaken place. And you, sir,' he turned to me, 'your name is Hannay. Mackinnon has warned me about you.'

'I'm glad that he remembers me,' I said with a sidelong glance at the gamekeeper. 'I have something to repay him for.'

'There will be no chance of that, not for the present at least. I have some quarters here where you won't be comfortable, but it will be a lot safer for you than running loose in the hills.'

He indicated one of the renovated cottages and Mackinnon made a move to escort us there.

We held our ground and Leithen rounded on our captor. 'I demand to see your prisoner, sir.'

'Demand, is it?' There was a cold humour about Kildennan now. 'You must think highly of yourself to be making demands.'

'I think highly of justice and the standards of civilised behaviour,' Leithen retorted. 'I wish to be assured that he is being properly treated.'

'He has been offered food and drink,' said Kildennan, 'though he has refused both. He has got the idea into his head that I mean to poison him.'

'That might be less cruel than whatever it is you do have in mind,' I put in.

Kildennan met my effrontery with a darkly raised

eyebrow. 'Let me tell you exactly what I have in mind. Do you see that oak there?'

I eyed the great tree that loomed over the ruins like a grieving giant, its gaunt branches casting crooked shadows on the barren ground.

'We see it,' Leithen acknowledged.

'Well, nigh on two hundred years ago, after the slaughter of Culloden, the Bonnie Prince was hidden away among these hills as he made his flight towards Skye.' He waved a hand towards the nearest slopes, as though we might still catch a glimpse of the fleeing Jacobites. 'The redcoats arrived, quite sure that the folk that dwelt here knew his hiding place. They ordered the people to betray their prince but they refused.

'So one by one the men were hanged from this very tree in expectation that, as the rope settled around his neck, one of them would lose his nerve and confess. None did. When all the men were dead, the women and children were driven into the hills to perish. Their homes were razed to the ground as a warning to all who would rise up against the German king who ruled them from London.

'Ever since, this place has been called *baile nam mairbh*, the Village of the Dead, and this oak known as *chraobh breitheanis*, the Judgement Tree. Many innocent men were hanged from its branches but now, at last, a guilty man shall swing there.'

The awful thought struck me that he was mixing up old wrongs with new to make himself an avenger of the ages. 'And you believe that ancient crime justifies you in carrying out a lynching?' I challenged him.

'There's to be no lynching,' Kildennan asserted angrily.

'He is on trial here as he should have been tried years ago.'

'A trial, eh?' said Leithen. 'Who might I ask is the judge? Where is the jury?'

'These men of mine are the jury,' Kildennan answered in a growl. 'I am his judge, as is my right by ancient custom.'

In spite of our bleak surroundings, Leithen had adopted his best barrister's manner. He addressed Kildennan as though he were facing the bench at the Old Bailey. 'And what is being set out by way of defence?'

'His only defence is whatever comes out of his mouth, and that has been little enough,' Kildennan replied contemptuously.

'So, trapped and half starved as he is, you expect him to conduct his own defence?' I said.

Kildennan's voice swelled like a rumble of thunder. 'I expect him to answer the charges, to admit his guilt. It's the last chance he will have to unburden his soiled conscience.'

'Then let us talk to him,' suggested Leithen. 'We might persuade him to speak up for himself.'

Even through the thickness of his beard I could see Kildennan's jaw clench as his eyes darted from us to his men to Christina. She met his gaze squarely while at the same time reaching down to scratch the head of her faithful hound.

'I'll talk to the prisoner and find out if he'll see you,' the laird conceded. 'It's possible he has no more interest in listening to you than I have.' He turned to his daughter with a wolfish smile. 'Kirsty, you'll keep a watch on them, eh?'

'Aye, Father, they'll not be taking a stroll.'

Kildennan returned to the cottage from which he had just emerged while Mackinnon stood guard at the door.

While the other three men watched us from a distance, we had the opportunity to converse with the formidable Christina. I had some hope that she might be persuaded to defect from her father's cause.

'Miss Kildennan, surely you – a woman – will not play along with this defacement of justice,' I appealed.

Christina bristled and the dog, sensing her mood, uttered a low growl deep in his throat. 'Just because my father calls me by that little girl's name, don't suppose my mettle is any less stern than his.'

'I never thought that for a moment,' I assured her. 'But will you make yourself a party to this wrong?'

A cold anger seized the young woman. 'Wrong? Why don't you go over to Belgium, find the bloody graves of my brothers, and tell them their father is wrong to bring their killer to justice.'

'This is not justice,' said Leithen, 'and I believe you know that. What your father intends will blight his life and yours for ever.'

Christina slammed the butt of her rifle down on the stony ground with a crack as hard as a gunshot. 'My life has been blighted already.'

Leithen and I were so taken aback by her vehemence we hardly knew what to say. In the face of our silence her cheek reddened and her eyes flashed vengefully.

'There's a reason I bind up my hair in this black ribbon. My dear Donnie and I had been married scarcely five weeks when he led a charge at the Somme. Straight into the hellish hail of machine guns he went and he was one of the first to fall. I doubt he even got so far as to see the faces of the Germans who were killing him. He was the bonniest laddie you ever could meet, with a ready smile and eyes as blue as the summer sky. And mild? Birds landed on his shoulder and the deer would come and eat from his hand. Much good any of that did him in the end.'

It was clear to me now that the stern aspect she presented to the world contained within it a raging blaze of injured spirit.

'We've all lost people.' Leithen spread his hands in an appeal for mercy. 'There's nobody left untouched by it all.'

'Yes, but some of us won't just swallow the loss like those cowards down in London,' Christina threw back at him. 'Some of us still burn with the wrong of it and no passage of time will quench that fire.'

'Believe me, we've both of us suffered our losses and witnessed terrible things we'll never forget,' I said. 'Ned here was gassed to the point of death on the very eve of the Armistice and it's little short of a miracle that he's not buried over there with so many others.'

Christina took pause and regarded Leithen closely.

'Yes, you have that look about you, Sir Edward.' Her voice almost caught in her throat. 'There's a shadow upon you that follows you still. You need to take care of yourself.'

Her sudden solicitude had softened her features, allowing me a momentary glimpse of the carefree girl she must once have been in the first flush of her love. Then in an instant it was gone. Her face hardened like a steel door slamming shut.

'Before the attack,' she said, 'Donnie wrote me a letter that only reached me after news had come of his death. When I opened it it was like hearing the voice of a ghost coming to me from a far-off land. He spoke of the bravery of his men, of their comradeship, and of the better world he was sure would come of all this. Where is that better world now, Mr Hannay?'

Before I could answer Kildennan reappeared and addressed us gruffly. 'Aye, he'll see you, for all the good it will do. I've no parson to offer him solace before the end, so I grant that privilege to you.'

7

THE KING IN CHECK

Leithen addressed our captor defiantly. 'I'm not looking to give him solace – I intend to mount a defence. He has a right to that much, doesn't he?'

Kildennan clenched his fists so tightly I could almost hear his knuckles crack. 'A defence, is it? Of *him*?'

I spoke up in support of Leithen's intent. 'If you're so certain of his guilt, then you surely can't be afraid of that.'

'Where he's concerned I have no fear at all, not of him, not of our own mealy-mouthed politicians, nor of anything you can find to say, Sir Edward. Go ahead and soak up his lies if you will. You'll not like the taste of them.'

He stood aside and waved us into the cottage where the prisoner was held. When we entered and our eyes adjusted to the dim light, we beheld a bare, unfurnished interior. There was some straw heaped up against the far wall and a bucket in the corner. The bars cemented into the window were clearly a recent addition. On the floor a plate of cold ham and a tin cup of water lay untouched.

Seated on the straw, with his legs stretched out before him and his head hung low, was the former Kaiser Wilhelm II, King of Prussia and Emperor of Germany. When he looked up, the hope that kindled in his eyes was almost pathetic.

'Ah, my friend, you live!' he exclaimed, struggling to his feet.

In his weakened state he lost his balance and would have fallen if I had not grasped his outstretched arm.

He patted me on the chest and smiled weakly. 'I feared you were dead, you my one friend in this savage country.'

'You have another friend, sir,' said Leithen quietly.

'This is Sir Edward Leithen,' I said. 'He is an eminent lawyer and between us we will do all that we can to get you out of here.'

'A lawyer?' Wilhelm appeared momentarily confused. 'My friend, that man out there is quite mad. He has confused me with some other person. I am, as I told you, an innocent Swiss tourist on whom fate has played a dastardly trick.'

'No, sir, I know who you are.' I spoke as kindly as I could. 'You are Wilhelm von Hohenzollern, the former Kaiser. I met you once when I was operating in your country under an assumed name. I recognised you yesterday when we met.'

Wilhelm's eyes drifted back and forth between us as he asked himself if we could be trusted.

'Denying your identity will gain you nothing,' said Leithen, 'not even time. Lord Kildennan knows very well who you are.'

'But how?' Wilhelm wondered haltingly. 'Who could have . . . ?'

His voice trailed away and I was afraid I would have to catch him again to keep him from swooning right in front of us. He recovered, however, and drew himself up in a show of injured dignity.

'Look, sir,' I appealed to him, 'it would be of some help if you could tell us how you come to be here in the first place.'

Wilhelm thrust the hand of his withered left arm into his pocket while with the other he rubbed his beard in a display of mental conflict.

'There was to be a meeting of persons sympathetic to my cause held in this obscure spot far from prying eyes,' he began at last. 'My adjutant, Captain von Ilsemann, and myself sailed here with my countryman Baron von Hilderling. When we landed, the baron's manservant Kurbin was waiting with a car. He drove us to a cottage here in the hills, where we were to be contacted by our other friends. When the captain and I awoke yesterday morning the baron and his man had vanished, taking their luggage with them.'

He hesitated and it was obvious that even now he was struggling to make sense of what had befallen him. 'I can only suppose the baron received warning of some threat against my person and made haste to head it off. Von Ilsemann and I separated and set out to search for them. That is when I ran into you, Mr Hannay.'

I met Leithen's eyes and knew he was thinking the same as I: that the Kaiser's own people had delivered him into the hands of his enemies for some dark purpose of their own.

'If you still have friends out there,' Leithen told his client, 'then so do we. We must do whatever we can to stall Kildennan's intent and hope that help is on the way.'

Wilhelm's lip curled contemptuously at the mention of his captor. 'He is obsessed, that one. Yes, he thinks we are still at war and that gives him some authority over me. He has none. All of this is a complete outrage!'

'Be that as it may, sir,' said Leithen, 'it is incumbent upon us to prepare some sort of defence.'

'Defence? You mean this is supposed to be some kind of trial?' Wilhelm scoffed. 'By what law does that brutish Scot think he can judge me?'

'I will do my best to dissuade him from this mad course,' said Leithen, 'I promise you that.'

The ex-Kaiser nodded grimly. 'He has shown me his ugly tree and made it clear that I have an appointment there. He has not even the decency simply to shoot me and call it murder.'

'Sir Edward has the most brilliant legal mind in the country,' I told Wilhelm, glad that he was showing some spirit. 'He will make a proper trial out of this and there's every chance he will win the case.'

'Yes, yes, a defence,' murmured the Kaiser absently.

'You must keep up your strength,' Leithen advised him. He took a sip from the cup of water and a nibble of the cold meat to prove that it was safe. The Kaiser smiled weakly and accepted the food and drink.

Leithen drew me aside and spoke confidentially.

'It's only for the sake of form that Kildennan has agreed to hear a defence. It's so he looks reasonable in the eyes of his men and keeps their respect, and so he can look his own face in the mirror after the deed is done. The sentence has already been decided, you see, and nothing I say is going to change that.'

'Then what are you going to do?' I asked.

His brow furrowed and he squeezed my arm. 'I'm going to play for time while we work out a plan of escape.'

At that moment Kildennan's large frame filled the doorway and we fell silent. 'So what's it to be?' he demanded gruffly. 'Does the prisoner wish you to speak on his behalf?'

Wilhelm faced his captor with a stiff show of dignity. 'If we must endure this nonsense, then I do. But I warn you again—'

'Wheesht with your warning,' Kildennan cut him off. 'Sir Edward, I grant you one hour with your client. After that, the trial will begin. We will not make it a long one, so your statement had best be brief. Mr Hannay, you will come with me.'

'I'd rather stay here with my friend,' I objected.

'I don't give a curse for your preferences,' the laird growled. 'Sir Edward has insisted on a role for himself which you, being no lawyer, have no part in.'

'I would like to have Mr Hannay here with me,' Leithen requested mildly.

Kildennan's eyes narrowed beneath his shaggy brows. 'I imagine you would. But I would be a fool to leave the three of you to conspire together. Come along, Hannay. If Sir Edward wishes to play the lawyer, that's his choice, but you have no business here other than as a bothersome bystander.'

When I made no move to leave, he gestured to his men who stood beyond the door. 'I'll have you dragged out if necessary.'

'There's no need for that,' said Leithen, laying a reassuring hand on my shoulder. 'You go ahead, Dick. I need to get on with establishing my case.'

Reluctantly I stepped outside and Mackinnon replaced the bar over the door. Christina, her rifle resting on her shoulder, observed the scene with an unhappy quirk of her mouth.

'You'll not harm these men, Father?' she asked. 'They've not done us any wrong.'

'They'll be perfectly safe so long as they do as they're told,' Kildennan replied. 'You understand that, Hannay? I'll let Sir Edward make his little speech, but that's the only concession I'll grant you. If you try to interfere in any way, the consequences will be on your own head.'

'I understand that,' I told him, 'but I have to say I'm sorry that you've implicated your daughter in all this.'

'I know where my duty lies,' Christina informed me sharply, 'and I'll carry it out as I see fit.'

'You'd best get back to the house, Kirsty,' said Kildennan, 'and keep an eye out for any more interlopers.'

There was a defiant gleam in the young woman's eye. 'I'll be more help to you here now that you have two more prisoners to guard.'

'We'll manage fine,' her father assured her. 'But I need you back home to stall anybody who comes looking for them. Now go!'

The last command was cold and impatient.

Christina lowered her eyes and bit her lip, holding in any words that might anger her father. Sensing her conflicted mood, the wolfhound rubbed his muzzle sympathetically against her leg.

'I'll go then,' she conceded. 'But mind you get it done swiftly and cleanly.'

She turned and strode off, sending Fearghal bounding on ahead of her.

Kildennan addressed me in an uncharacteristically hushed voice. 'She has a warrior's soul, Hannay, but she's still a woman. I'll not make her witness the grisly end of all this. I'll see she comes out of it clear of any blame.'

His obvious affection for his daughter gave me hope that he was capable of other humane feeling and might yet be deflected from his cruel purpose.

I was placed inside one of the partially intact hovels where I was given food and water which I consumed under the watchful eye of the cadaverous guard, whose rifle was pointed at me the whole time. It was frustrating not to be able to discuss our situation with Leithen and seek some way of extricating ourselves and the ex-Kaiser. There was little chance we would be able to overcome our armed captors. They were hard-bitten men and completely devoted to their laird. My one hope was that Leithen might summon the eloquence to weaken their resolve.

Such were my thoughts when I was summoned forth to take my place in Kildennan's makeshift courtroom.

8

A SURPRISED WITNESS

The court Kildennan had set up in the centre of the village consisted of some benches and a few rickety wooden tables. The laird, in his capacity of judge, sat beneath the towering oak with the jury to his left. This consisted of three men who, contrary to normal legal practice, were all armed. To the judge's right sat the prisoner with myself on one side and Leithen on the other.

Kildennan introduced the jurymen by name: Hamish Mackinnon, Peter Strachan, who was young Roddy's father, and Hugh Anderson, the gaunt-faced man who had stood guard over me. Roddy was stationed some distance off to keep watch against any intrusion.

Kildennan glowered at our bench as he declared his tribunal to be in session. He then gestured to Mackinnon, who stood up and read from a sheet of paper he held at arm's length before him.

'Under the terms of the Versailles treaty the German government accepted their responsibility for the loss and damage suffered by allied governments and populations imposed by the aggression of Germany and her allies.'

Leithen stood and raised a hand to silence the gamekeeper. 'Any admissions made by the German government are irrelevant,' he stated. 'It is universally accepted that an extorted confession is worthless. A man will admit to anything if you put a gun to his head.'

'Sit down!' Kildennan roared, slamming a fist on the

table before him. 'Germany's war guilt is an established fact that will not be disputed here. You will have your say at the proper time, Leithen.'

Leithen quietly resumed his seat and received an approving nod from the ex-Kaiser. I knew what a delicate game he must play. He needed to drag out this trial as long as possible, but if he tested Kildennan's patience too far, the laird was likely to cut straight to the verdict and the execution. If not for our intervention it was likely that the prisoner would already be dead.

Mackinnon resumed the reading of the charges as they had been laid out in brief in the Treaty of Versailles. They were: One, that of starting an aggressive war against Russia, France and other countries. Two, violating the neutrality of Belgium and Luxembourg which had been guaranteed by treaty. Three, ordering the violation of the laws and customs of war, especially in Belgium, France and Poland. Four, declaring unlimited submarine warfare. Five, ordering the violation of the laws and customs of war in this submarine campaign.

When the gamekeeper sat down, Kildennan scowled at us and said, 'How does the accused plead?'

Leithen stood and spoke in a flat, unemotional voice, designed to avoid any provocation. 'My client does not recognise the right of this unauthorised tribunal to try him.'

Kildennan greeted this with crude laughter, but Leithen continued in the same even tone.

'Such a view is only to be expected, considering his former position, but I will speak on his behalf and present his case to the court.'

'You can speak your piece when I call upon you,'

Kildennan stated scornfully, waving him back down. 'First we'll have the case for the prosecution.'

The grizzled Strachan now stood. I wondered if all three jury members had suffered in the war, either through personal injury or family loss. This man certainly had a vengeful look to him as he began a grim litany of German atrocities. He needed no paper to read from, for these crimes seemed to be etched into his heart. They included the shooting of hostages, the demolition of civilian houses with resultant loss of life, the sinking of civilian vessels, and other violations with which I was familiar.

I could see Wilhelm becoming increasingly impatient with the relentless roll of accusations. His heel ground into the earth, his fingers clutched at the hem of his jacket and he mouthed many silent curses I was glad not to hear. Finally his outrage overcame him and he started to rise from his seat. Before he could speak, Leithen grabbed him by the arm and pulled him back down.

'Hold your peace, sir,' he urged. 'Our turn will come soon enough.'

I understood, as Leithen did, that every second we could drag this matter out increased, however infinitesimally, our chance of rescue. Let his accusers take their full measure of time to set out their case.

The ex-Kaiser's beard appeared to bristle and he clenched his teeth tight against the words of protest welling up in his heart. His grey eyes had swelled almost to the point of bulging out of his head. Fortunately Leithen's soothing admonitions of forbearance had their effect. His client wiped a kerchief across his brow and calmed himself with several deep breaths.

Kildennan fixed a hostile glare on his prisoner, which carried an implicit threat of how any future interruption would be dealt with. At the same time I could not help but sense that he gained a certain satisfaction from seeing his foe so incensed.

Finally the accuser sat down, only to be replaced by the pale-faced Anderson whose jaw quivered as he outlined how Wilhelm II had driven the world to war. He had ordered the expansion of the German army and fleet with the clear intention of extending his power by both land and sea. He had made numerous bellicose speeches, sought out occasions for conflict with the other European powers, and egged on his own generals and admirals with his rampant militarism. On this count he was personally responsible for every drop of blood spilled, including that of his own people, and the world must see that a man could not bring down hell upon the earth and walk away unscathed.

With that final flourish the man sat down and a few moments of sombre silence ensued. The former Kaiser's eyes were downcast, fixed on his knotted fingers. He was either doing his best to control himself as Leithen had instructed, or he had shut himself off from the horrific predicament into which he had stumbled so unwisely.

At last Kildennan gestured towards our bench and rumbled, 'Sir Edward.'

Leithen rose and walked into the centre of the court. He appeared in no way daunted by the impossibility of his task and stood before the jury in an attitude of righteous dignity. He began by questioning the legality of this court, wondering how men of conscience could set aside the laws of their own country and prepare themselves to do murder.

Kildennan cut him off with a bellow. 'This court is convened under the ancient laws of our clan, Sir Edward, so you can cease your lawyerly claptrap and get to the meat of the matter. Have you anything to say to mitigate the weighty and obvious guilt of your client?'

'I would say that if anyone here wishes to see justice done,' Leithen retorted, 'he will hand the prisoner over to the proper authorities and let the matter proceed in an honest and legal way.'

'Sir Edward, if you challenge the authority of this court once more,' Kildennan warned darkly, 'you and your friend Hannay will be removed and we will press on more swiftly to a verdict without you.'

There was a brief pause before Leithen lowered his head respectfully. 'As the court wishes,' he conceded mildly.

He proceeded with his case, pointing out that, as many of us knew, the more grotesque accounts of early German atrocities in Belgium – mutilations, the slaughter of children, and other such horrors – were pure fabrication, intended to instil in our people a fervour for a war whose root causes remained obscure to many of them.

'There were genuine crimes committed,' he conceded, 'but these were the acts of individual officers and were not carried out by command of their king.'

Kildennan drummed his fingers impatiently on the table before him. It was clear he regarded the defence as a futile waste of his time, but he had agreed to let Leithen have his say, and, unyielding as he was in so many ways, he was not a man to go back on his word.

Now Leithen spoke in general terms of the inevitable horrors of war, the unavoidable civilian casualties, how men under the pressure of bombardment and the constant threat of death often lost many of the civilised constraints that normally guided them.

'Even on the British side,' he said, 'there were accusations of misconduct. These included the execution of survivors of the destroyed U-boat U-27, who were shot at the order of—'

He was silenced by a roar from Kildennan.

'I'll not hear you defame our brave boys,' his face was filled with thunder, 'boys like my Calum and my wee Ronald, who died courageously to save the world from this man's arrogant lust for power.' He surged to his feet and crashed both fists down on his table. 'You'd best change your tack right now if you have any consideration for your client, and for your own safety too.'

It was a dangerous moment and I noticed the eyes of the jurymen flickering back and forth between Leithen and their chief to see how the balance would tilt. Kildennan was clearly poised to respond to any further provocation with a murderous fury.

'I accept the court's rebuke,' said Leithen humbly. 'I have no wish to cause offence and I withdraw my last remark.'

I was amazed and admiring of how quickly Leithen could choose the right response to keep our perilous situation from sliding into immediate catastrophe. It was as if he were picking his way through a minefield, and whenever his foot hovered over an explosive he was able, by some uncanny instinct, to sidestep it at the last possible instant.

When Kildennan sat down, Leithen resumed his defence. He spoke now of how the world was guided by huge cultural and economic forces, how one man, however exalted his rank, had only the most limited influence over the course of history. Mankind itself, he said, marked as we were with the taint of original sin, was responsible for so much wrong. Historical crimes on the scale of those described in this court today could not be ascribed to the agency of one individual.

The jurors had listened attentively, little inclined as they might be to act upon Leithen's words. There was in Kildennan's eye a certain glint of respect for the lawyer's eloquence, but I knew that Cicero himself could not muster a case to divert him from his deathly purpose.

'If you are finished, Sir Edward, we shall proceed to the verdict,' the laird announced sonorously.

Leithen appeared to consider for a moment before coming to a decision.

'If it please the court,' he said, 'I am not yet done.'

Kildennan stood and scowled warningly. 'I think, Sir Edward, we have granted you enough leeway. We have listened to your arguments and we are done with them.'

'I understand that,' said Leithen, 'and I am not asking you to listen to me any longer. I wish to call a witness.'

'A witness?' Kildennan was baffled and astounded.

'I believe that is my right,' Leithen asserted.

'Right or no,' said the laird, 'how in the name of all that's holy do you mean to lay your hands on a witness?'

'I have one right here,' said Leithen, turning to me. 'I call to the stand General Sir Richard Hannay.'

9

THE VERDICT

I was as stunned as our Highland captors to hear myself called as a witness. With a flick of his wrist Leithen motioned me to stand and join him. I realised Kildennan was caught between his impatience to pass sentence and curiosity as to what my testimony would be. We had to move quickly if we were to turn this moment of indecision to our advantage.

Rising, I walked briskly to Leithen's side. I saw the jurymen shake their heads, but whether in disapproval of my friend's delaying tactics or in admiration for his audacity, I could not tell.

Leithen addressed me with great formality. 'You are General Sir Richard Hannay, late of the Lennox Highlanders?'

'I am,' I answered just as stiffly.

I saw Kildennan hesitate and sway slightly on his feet before sitting down. I suppressed a sigh of relief. The trial would continue.

'Your record in the Great War is well known,' said Leithen, 'so we'll set that aside for now. Before coming to Britain you lived most of your life in South Africa.'

'Yes,' I confirmed. 'I was born here in Scotland but the family moved to South Africa when I was six.'

'And you worked there as a mining engineer.'

'That's right. I spent some years prospecting for copper in Damaraland and made a fair sum for myself in Bulawayo.'

Leithen continued in the same matter-of-fact tone. 'You also had a military career.'

'I did fight in the Matabele Wars,' I acknowledged. I guessed that he was attempting to establish my credibility. 'I served two years with the Imperial Light Horse.'

'You also served in the Boer War. Is that correct?'

'It is. I was an intelligence officer at Delagoa Bay.'

'In that role you were well informed about the conduct of the war in all its aspects.'

'I suppose so.'

I wasn't sure where my friend was aiming with this line of questioning, but I was prepared to play my part if it would extend the trial to nightfall and perhaps beyond. Leithen, I knew, was seeking some means to wrest the life of his client from Kildennan's determined grasp, which was as delicate and difficult an operation as trying to coax a cut of raw meat away from a hungry tiger.

Leithen turned to face me. 'You are aware then that certain units on our side violated the rules of warfare?'

The question gave me pause. Keeping one eye on Kildennan to see how he would react, I answered guardedly, 'I believe that is the case.'

'In fact,' said Leithen, in a voice heavy with regret, 'they executed prisoners and carried out revenge killings.'

I shifted my feet uncomfortably as memories came back to me of those harrowing times. I felt compelled to stand up for our troops, many of whom had been personal friends.

'Yes, I know. But those were not regular British soldiers,' I explained. 'They were mounted irregulars, the Bushveldt Carbineers they were called.'

'Nonetheless these crimes were committed.'

I noticed Kildennan leaning forward, ready to pounce on any incautious word he saw as violating the rules of his makeshift court. I knew I had to be quick in my response. 'The men who committed them were court martialled,' I informed the jurymen. 'Some were executed for what they had done. Justice was done.'

The invocation of the word *justice* appeared to appease Kildennan's simmering impatience – at least for the moment. He settled himself back in his seat with an approving nod.

I became aware that Leithen was proceeding. 'Yes, the men who committed those acts, some of them at least, were punished.' He paused to allow the point to sink in before putting his next question. 'Was anyone in the higher command ever held accountable for what those men did?'

I began to see where he was leading with this line of questioning and it made me distinctly uneasy. There were matters it gave me no pleasure to recall. 'No, those were the actions of a few individuals. It was no part of our military policy.'

'Of course it wasn't,' Leithen agreed. 'And I'm sure it could be argued that those individuals felt themselves provoked by what they perceived as unlawful actions on the part of the enemy.'

'Such things happen in war,' I admitted. 'Any war.'

'A fact that everyone here is well aware of,' Leithen noted.

I could tell that he was trying to form some sort of consensus between ourselves and our captors, and he certainly had the attention of the jurors.

'A number of Boer farms were destroyed, I believe,' Leithen continued, almost casually, as if the thought had just occurred to him. 'In fact, crops were burned, cattle slaughtered, fields salted and wells poisoned.'

'With good reason,' I felt compelled to say. 'This was a war like none that had gone before.'

'No?' Leithen used that one word like a sharp probe.

'The Boers fought a campaign of concealment and ambush,' I explained. 'Never a battle, only hit and run raids. They would strike then melt away into the bush before our men could come to grips with them.'

'There is no doubt our forces were in a difficult position,' Leithen concurred. 'And the farms . . . ?'

'As the Boer commandos would not come to battle, it was decided that the only way to combat them was to remove their source of supplies.'

'It was a matter of military necessity, then.'

'It was.' Those two words left a bitter taste in my mouth.

Leithen made a silent circuit of the court area, as if awaiting some reaction from our captors. Despite my own misgivings, I marvelled at the way he had shifted the ground of his defence to an earlier conflict. It was a tactic designed to redistribute the blame for the ugly tragedies of war. Whether or not Kildennan would be swayed by this remained to be seen.

With half an eye on the jury, my friend resumed. 'Women and children were displaced from those farms, of course. Was any provision made for them?'

'They were taken to camps,' I replied. 'They would not

have been left to starve.'

'Yes, camps.' Leithen rubbed his chin meditatively, allowing another long pause. 'As well as farms, I believe towns were also destroyed.'

I wished I could keep silent, but I had to follow Leithen's lead. 'One or two,' I admitted.

'The Boer town of Ventersburg was razed to the ground,' said Leithen, restricting himself to a flat tone without drama, 'every building, including the church. The town of Louis Trichardt was also burned down. What became of all those people left homeless – those tens of thousands of women and children and the elderly? Were they also placed in camps?'

I could find no words to answer. My reluctant nod had to suffice.

The jurymen were showing signs of discomfort, shifting in their seats, clearing their throats. Kildennan sat motionless. His face was dark with displeasure, but having allowed Leithen to come this far, the laird felt compelled to let him continue.

In the same dry, dispassionate tone Leithen enquired, 'What were conditions like in those camps, General Hannay?'

I remembered reports that described the squalor and meagre rations, and how efforts to improve matters had been hindered by the necessity of maintaining supplies to our troops in the field.

'I believe they were quite harsh,' I answered at last. 'There were so many people and resources were scarce. There was only so much food and medicine.'

My head was beginning to throb and my palms

sweated as if I were the accused and my own life were on the line. There was a tension in the air that seemed to still the noise of the birds and quiet the rustling of the breeze.

'That's understandable,' said Leithen. His voice grew deceptively softer as he took the next fateful step. 'I suppose, under the circumstances, a few civilian deaths were inevitable.'

I had to struggle to raise my voice above a whisper. 'Yes, they were.'

'Could you estimate, General Hannay, how many civilians died in those camps?'

I lowered my eyes to the ground and shook my head.

Leithen's voice had now taken on an authority that held everyone present in its grip. Even Kildennan seemed frozen to the spot as my friend approached the climax of his argument.

'Would it surprise you to learn that the numbers were upward of twenty thousand?'

'I couldn't deny that. I wouldn't even try to.'

Having held himself in check for so long, Leithen now assumed the righteous bearing of a man faced with an offence against civilisation itself.

'General Hannay, what do you yourself feel about this policy that drove so many to their deaths?'

I looked up and met his gaze, wishing I did not have to.

'It was a damned dirty business. I wish we'd had no part in it.'

Leithen swung around to face Kildennan. 'A damned dirty business,' he repeated. With his eyes still fixed squarely on the laird, he addressed a final question to me.

'Was anyone ever held to account for all those thousands of deaths?'

'No,' I answered hoarsely, 'no one ever was.'

Kildennan did not stand but he swelled up with rage. 'Is this your defence, Sir Edward, to blacken the reputation of your own country?'

Leithen was now immovable. 'Do you deny the truth of what I have stated? Do you deny even one word of it?'

Kildennan fulminated wordlessly as Leithen turned on the jury. 'Is any man, is any country, so utterly without sin that they have the right to cast the first stone? For the love of God, will you men show a little humility?'

Such was the strength of Leithen's conviction at this point, I was certain one or two of his audience were wavering. Then disaster struck.

While his defender's back was turned to him, Wilhelm leapt up and took three steps forward, his head held high, his arms gesturing wildly.

'Yes, it is as he says,' he declared, shaking his fist at Kildennan. 'By what right do you dare to stand judgement over me? It was England that started the war. You armed your soldiers, you created your vast Navy. For what? For amusement? No! To turn them both on Germany because you could not abide a rival to your ambitions.'

Leithen whipped around in horror and signalled the ex-Kaiser to be still, but it was too late. If he had achieved anything at all it was now being recklessly undone.

Kildennan rose. 'The prisoner will return to his place.' The order was shockingly calm, as if he were not at all upset at the ex-Kaiser's outburst. In fact he seemed relieved that by his own foolishness the old man had drawn attention away from Leithen's humane appeal and back upon himself.

'I will not be silent!' Wilhelm stamped his foot on the ground and his eyes bulged horribly in the extremity of his offended pride. 'You seize me like brigands, shut me up in that filthy hole, and you play at being judges and juries. God Himself set me upon the throne and only God Himself will judge me!'

'He will that,' Kildennan agreed coldly. 'I will set you before him now. Gentlemen of the jury, how do you find the accused?'

One after another, their words like the tolling of a terrible bell, the jurymen answered, 'Guilty!'

'Yes, you are guilty,' Kildennan directed the full force of his hatred at his prisoner, 'guilty of deaths uncounted, of causing suffering unmerited, and you have delivered yourself into the hands of men who curse your name. I sentence you to death by hanging, sentence to be carried out at once.'

Mackinnon and Strachan advanced to restrain the accused while Anderson covered me with his rifle. As Kildennan grabbed hold of his own gun Leithen placed himself directly between him and the ex-Kaiser, who was still trembling in his rage.

'It is you who will be damned,' the old man fumed at his accuser, 'damned for this sacrilege!'

Leithen leaned across the judge's table to make a last desperate appeal. 'You cannot drag him to his death in this condition,' he pleaded. 'For mercy's sake give him the night to make his peace with God. As a Christian you cannot deny him that.'

A slow, wolfish smile spread across the laird's face. 'Very well. Let him spend his last night on earth in contemplation of what awaits him with the dawn.'

He indicated the deathly tree that loomed behind him as his men seized the ex-Kaiser and bundled him back to his wretched cell.

PAWN SACRIFICE

The same morning that a group of strangers set out to rescue his master, Captain Sigurd von Ilsemann slowly awoke from a drug-induced slumber. His head was still thick with the effects of chloroform and when he cracked his eyes open they filled with a dull blur of light. He could feel at once that his wrists and ankles were bound and that he was in effect a prisoner. Struggling to disperse the fog from his brain, he tried to piece together how he came to find himself in this situation.

He remembered oversleeping the previous morning and finding that Baron von Hilderling and his man had vanished without a word. The Kaiser scornfully dismissed his adjutant's suspicion that the two of them had been drugged somehow and insisted they split up to make a search for their missing companions.

After a futile tramp around the wooded hills, he made his way back to the cottage to discover that the Kaiser had not returned. He immediately set out to search in the other direction, but quickly became lost among the gullies and tangles of this undomesticated country.

It was almost by accident that he stumbled back upon the cottage hours later. Throwing open the door, he dashed inside, hoping to find the emperor safely returned. Instead, as soon as he stepped into the front room, he was seized by the shoulder and twisted roughly around. Angrily he knocked aside the clutching fingers and raised a hand to defend himself. Before he could strike a blow he heard the voice of Baron von Hilderling. 'Gently, Hauptmann von Ilsemann. We are your good friends.'

Now he saw that he had been grabbed by the baron's heavy-set minion Kurbin. The expression on the man's face had little about it of friendship. Standing by the fireplace was the baron, with one hand in the pocket of his long coat and the other holding a scented cigarette. He was a big man with a small round head set atop a thick neck. There was a rough animal energy about him, like that of an untamed bull, so that he seemed almost at home in this untamed landscape.

'Where have you been?' Ilsemann demanded. 'Why did you sneak away in the night like thieves?'

The baron appeared genuinely taken aback by the question. 'Hauptmann, we left to make preparations for the important conference that is the whole purpose of this enterprise.' He took a long draw on his cigarette and expelled the smoke in a leisurely cloud. 'The Kaiser was clearly exhausted from the strain of the journey and I deemed it most considerate to wake neither of you.'

It sounded perfectly plausible, but Ilsemann was suspicious. Before he could find sufficient grounds to voice his doubts, however, the baron asked, 'And where is His Majesty? Is he following along behind you? You should not have let him venture outdoors.'

'He insisted that we search for you,' Ilsemann retorted with some bitterness. 'We were to go in separate directions and meet back at the cottage, but he has not returned.'

'That was very foolish of you,' Hilderling chided him. 'You should have remained here awaiting our return.' He casually let his cigarette drop into the grate.

'This entire situation is of your making,' Ilsemann accused him. 'What are we to do now? We cannot leave the emperor alone among these foreigners.'

'The situation is serious,' the baron agreed. 'Listen, we have already transferred all your baggage into my car and I have taken rooms at the local spa. We will go there to make our plans. I have friends I can contact who will do all in their power to aid us.'

'Do you mean *him*?' Ilsemann pressed, referring to the high-born Englishman who had been the prime guarantor of the emperor's safety. 'Has he arrived yet?'

'I expect him at any moment,' the baron assured him. 'Believe me, this affair is in very good hands. Come, you need food and a chance to refresh yourself. My car is just beyond the trees.'

They walked together to where the green Daimler was parked on a rough dirt track. As he climbed into the passenger seat Ilsemann was surprised to see the baron take the wheel while the thick-set Kurbin slid into the back.

'Baron, we must abandon this reckless enterprise,' Ilsemann said as they wove their way through the hills. 'It was doomed from the start and now it has gone wrong before even reaching the first hurdle.'

'Your assessment is overly pessimistic,' said Hilderling soberly. 'But I agree that we need a change of plan.'

Suddenly Ilsemann was seized from behind and a cloth soaked in chloroform was pressed hard against his face. He struggled futilely, trying not to breathe in the fumes, but succumbed within a minute, cursing himself for his carelessness. His final thought as the darkness closed in was that he had foolishly betrayed the emperor into the hands of his enemies.

Now, as his senses returned, he became gradually aware that he was stretched out on a bed in a simply furnished hotel room. His wrists were tied behind his back and his ankles were also bound together. As he stirred, a pair of powerful hands seized him roughly by the shoulders, dragged him from the bed and planted him on a wooden chair.

Baron von Hilderling was seated opposite him, noting his recovery with interest. When Ilsemann felt himself droop, the baron placed a fist under his chin and forced his head up, assessing his condition.

'We have kept you sedated overnight, Hauptmann von Ilsemann, but now it is time for you to wake. We have much to talk about. In the meantime I recommend that you not cry out or make any sort of fuss. You do not wish to provoke Kurbin.'

Ilsemann could see Kurbin only a few feet away, standing by a curtained window, playing with a small-bladed knife. The baron's henchman had the sly look of a killer and Ilsemann had no doubt that if he called for help his throat would be cut in an instant.

'What are we doing here?' The dryness in his throat made Ilsemann cough. 'Why are we not searching for the emperor?'

'There is no need for a search,' Hilderling replied. 'I know exactly where he is.'

Ilsemann attempted a few tentative tugs against the cords binding him and discovered that he was quite helpless. He saw a satisfied smirk cross Kurbin's heavy face and knew that it was he who had bound him with such efficiency.

'Please do not injure yourself,' said Hilderling with cold solicitude. 'I am sure you are uncomfortable enough without any sprains or pulled muscles.'

Ilsemann's brain whirred with urgent thoughts, trying to spin sense from this confusion. 'Very well, where is the emperor?'

'He is in the hands of a man who does not wish him well,' answered the baron in a tone of unconvincing regret, 'a Scottish lord named Kildennan. I met him last year in London at a meeting of those who seek a new order in Europe, one that will restore discipline to our societies and drive back the scourge of Bolshevism. Our conversation turned to matters of justice, and knowing his intent, I arranged for him to take possession of his hated enemy. I am afraid the Kaiser's life has fallen forfeit to the greater scheme of things.'

Ilsemann's chest swelled with indignation and he struggled to keep his voice under control. 'You are a member of one of our oldest families, an officer sworn to uphold the interests of his country.'

'That is precisely what I am doing.'

'By betraying your emperor? If I were not tied I would teach you a lesson in honour.'

Kurbin made to pick up a bottle and a cloth from a nearby table but Hilderling signalled him to stop. 'We do not want Hauptmann von Ilsemann unconscious for now. I wish him to understand.'

'To understand that you are in the employ of our enemies? What are they paying you?'

Hilderling sighed. 'You are an idealistic fellow, Hauptmann, with some admirable qualities, but you are naïve. Let me explain to you the reality of politics in our world today. Have you heard of the Iron Hand?'

'It is some sort of club for ex-military officers, is it not?'

'On the surface, yes. But there is an inner circle with loftier aims than drinking schnapps and reminiscing about old battles. We believe in learning from past mistakes and building a new road to a glorious future. Some of us joined Hugo Stinnes' party, sharing his desire to lead Germany out of the ruin of the war.'

Ilsemann had met Stinnes on one of his visits to the homeland and had been impressed with the late industrialist's sincere desire to support the ex-Kaiser and to restore Germany to greatness.

'I do not believe that Hugo Stinnes would play any part in what you are doing,' he stated firmly.

'Stinnes was quite sincere in his aim of returning Wilhelm to the throne,' Hilderling agreed, 'and it was on that basis he used his contacts and his influence to lay the groundwork for the meeting that brought us all here. His plan was that interested parties from both Germany and Britain would gather in this remote spot to form a plan of action for restoring the German monarchy.'

A horrifying thought struck Ilsemann. 'Stinnes' death then – it was not an accident?'

'Whether an accident or not,' Hilderling shrugged, 'it left the way open for me to step in and take charge of the whole endeavour, diverting it to more practical ends.'

Ilsemann was contemptuous. 'And what might those be?'

'You surely are not ignorant of the many assassinations and attempted coups that have plagued our country over the past few years,' said the baron. 'If this continues, everything we hold dear will fall prey to the zealots of communism and anarchy. A firm hand is needed, one that will pull together all the elements of our divided society.'

'In that case, what is to be gained by abandoning the emperor?' Ilsemann appealed. 'Surely he is that man by the authority of history and tradition.'

'The Kaiser can never again lead Germany,' said Hilderling. 'He has not enough support in the country, nor does he have the necessary qualities to gain that support. But he can serve an even greater purpose – as a martyr.'

A cold wave of shock passed over Ilsemann. 'What in God's name are you talking about?'

'Suppose he came to this country in good faith, with assurances of safety from someone in the highest echelons of the British state.' Hilderling rose to his feet and lit a cigarette as he spoke. 'Suppose then he was seized and killed on this very soil by men crazed with the desire for vengeance. What do you think the reaction in Germany would be?'

Ilsemann shook his head at the dreadful prospect. 'It scarcely bears thinking about.'

'Monarchists would rise up in arms,' Hilderling went on, 'and even those who despised the old Kaiser would be outraged at such an affront. Do you not think the whole country would be ready to unite behind one leader, behind a man with the determination to restore our national honour?'

'There is no one who could command such authority,' Ilsemann told him. 'Stinnes is dead and most of our politicians are discredited.'

'We already have our eye on such a man, Hauptmann.' There was a chilling hint of triumph in the baron's voice. 'It is simply a matter of timing.'

'And for the sake of this putative saviour,' Ilsemann accused him, 'you would betray your emperor.'

'Do you want to watch him rot away year after year in that Dutch kennel?' the baron demanded. 'Or would you rather see him suffer a noble martyrdom and his name be glorified for ever?'

'You have a curious concept of glory, Herr Baron.'

Hilderling stood directly in front of Ilsemann and glowered down at him. 'You have one last chance now, Hauptmann, to abandon an outdated and useless loyalty. I offer you a role in the new reality, a respected place in the future Germany.'

Ilsemann felt his head swimming. He had faced death more than once in the war and he preferred that to denying his master. The thought passed briefly across his mind that he might lie, play for time, pretend to cooperate in hope of finding an opportunity to escape, but as he gazed up at his captor he knew the baron would not be fooled by false words.

'I do not believe I wish to live in your new Germany, baron,' he answered with stony calm, 'nor do I want any part of your treason.'

'In the game of the world such moves are often a necessity,' said Hilderling. 'What does it say in Scripture? That one man must die for the good of the people.'

'The man who said that was not one of the saints,' Ilsemann retorted bitterly. 'He was Caiaphas, the high priest.'

'Those of us burdened with the fate of nations do not have the luxury of sainthood,' Hilderling sneered. 'To do what we must requires that we get dirt on our hands, and sometimes blood.'

'Herr Baron,' Kurbin interjected, 'what are we to do with this stubborn man?'

Hilderling blew a stream of scented cigarette smoke into the face of his captive. 'I am afraid, Hauptmann, that you are only a pawn in this affair and sometimes a pawn must be sacrificed.'

PART TWO

A SPOT OF POACHING

10

THE RULES OF THE GAME

Having already surveyed the area for sporting purposes, Lamancha and Palliser-Yeates had no trouble finding their way to the place where the Kaiser had been staying. Perched on high ground and overshadowed by dark pines, the building was an uncompromising rectangular block with a hipped roof and small windows like squinting eyes. A peeling sign over the door read *Briar Cottage*.

'It's not exactly a palace,' Lamancha commented drily.

'Yes, it looks about as inviting as an abandoned byre,' Palliser-Yeates agreed. 'I suppose the Kaiser was willing to sacrifice comfort for the sake of anonymity.'

He rapped loudly on the door but there was no response. They waited for a few seconds before Lamancha gave it a shove; it swung open easily.

'I suppose we'd best have a look at the royal accommodations,' he said, stepping over the threshold.

Once inside, they made a quick exploration. The rooms were sparsely furnished, as though the owner begrudged anything other than the most basic of amenities. The place had been swept recently and the beds stripped.

'You'd be forgiven for thinking nobody had stayed here at all,' said Lamancha.

They found their way to the kitchen where Lamancha flung open the empty cupboards and drawers while Palliser-Yeates examined the stove. The meticulousness that had served him so well in his banking business impelled him to pick up a set of coal tongs and poke among the ashes in the grate.

'Aha! Here's something,' he announced, plucking out a charred fragment of greased paper and displaying it to his friend.

Lamancha peered closely. 'It looks like the stuff grocers use to wrap butter and cheese.'

Palliser-Yeates turned the fragment over. 'There's some lettering here – something *Food* then *K-i-n-c-l-a . . .*'

'Kinclavers, that town at the head of the glen,' said Lamancha. 'It's about twelve miles from here.'

'Our friends must have collected their supplies from a grocer's shop there,' said Palliser-Yeates.

Lamancha pondered a moment. 'We should head over there and try to pick up their trail.'

'And perhaps stop for a spot of lunch?' Palliser-Yeates suggested.

Lamancha clapped his friend on the shoulder. 'You see, John, being back in the game has already given you a healthy appetite. Let's head down to the main road and see if we can't get a lift into town.'

Leaving the empty cottage, the two men set off down the slope. The sunlight slanting through the pines dappled the needle-strewn ground and a resiny scent filled the air. Lamancha began to whistle 'Lilliburlero', setting his rifle across his shoulder like a trooper on parade.

Palliser-Yeates's mood was considerably less jaunty.

'I appreciate that this is the sort of lark you thrive on, Charles,' he said, 'but I'm more than a little concerned about this particular game. Last time out we could count on the other fellow not to be trigger happy and gun us down. But now, how do we know the rules of civilised behaviour still apply? Can we be sure that the cards haven't been tossed in the air to land where they will?'

Lamancha ceased his whistling. 'Hang it all, John, even if Kildennan does fancy himself as some kind of old style Highland chieftain, he's still just as British as we are and probably went to the same sort of school. You don't shake off all that, not when it's been drummed into you for years.'

'But what about the Germans?' Palliser-Yeates pressed. 'I don't think their Prussian military academies hold to the same notions of fair play as Eton and Harrow.'

Lamancha swatted a low-hanging branch out of his way with the barrel of his rifle. 'Look, whoever they turn out to be, patriots or villains, your German never loses his sense of discipline and order. That's something you can depend on.'

'I'm just asking you to bear in mind that this lot may have had a hand in turning their own man over to an enemy,' Palliser-Yeates reminded his companion. 'If so, they must be a pretty unscrupulous bunch.'

'Granted they may be a rough crew, but they're not going to go off half-cocked in a foreign land where they could so easily fall foul of the law.'

'I don't know, John,' said Palliser-Yeates, 'I sometimes get the awful feeling that with the war honour itself has been broken, like a sword shattered on a rock.'

Lamancha sought to alleviate his friend's pessimism with a hearty slap on the back. 'John, as long as there are sound chaps like yourself to depend on, the old world will struggle through even the worst of its troubles.' Suddenly he pointed with his rifle. 'Look, there's the road below – and I swear I can hear a car coming.'

Sir Archibald Roylance had only been the MP for Wester Ross for a matter of months, but he was already glad of any excuse to escape the ghastly confines of the Mother of Parliaments. He would rather be sent back in time to endure the hardship of the trenches once more than face another ten minutes of the Chief Whip's eloquently expressed displeasure. A timely meeting with representatives of the fishing industry in Lochinver was like a pleasant cocktail party by comparison and happily coincided with an opportunity to reunite with three old friends to celebrate the anniversary of their notorious exploits as John Macnab. As he barrelled west along the road from Kinclavers towards Rushforth Lodge, he hoped he hadn't missed the reunion.

While he was not deemed an official Macnab, it was a few incautious words of Archie's concerning his old pal Jim Tarras that had inspired the whole jape and he had been increasingly drawn into the adventure, not only through loyalty to his friends, but because of meeting the wonderful Janet Raden. Her father's estate was one of those to be plundered by the cunning poacher, but after successfully defending her home ground, she had joined the cause of Macnab. From being a companion in that adventure, Janet had by some miracle become a wife of whom he would never believe himself worthy. Archie knew that he, more than any of the others, had reason to celebrate last year's madcap exploits.

He had thrown the top down on his precious Hispana

as it roared along the narrow Highland roads. The car's aluminium straight-six engine was based on an aircraft design, and the breeze buffeting his face as he sped along made him feel as though he were once again flying his old Shark-Gladas above the battle-scarred countryside of France.

As he whipped the speeding vehicle around a tight turn, narrowly missing an errant goat, he threw a sidelong glance at his bride, wondering at the ardent blue eyes behind those dark lashes and the sunlight sparking flashes of gold from her bright blonde hair. She was a magical creature, he reflected dreamily, who brought the light of another world to burst upon the eyes of men.

Most of Archie's friends refused to ride with him in his favourite car, claiming that he drove as though he were performing a series of aerial corkscrews in the middle of a dogfight. They were convinced that he was destined one day for an almighty smash. Only Janet delighted in his fearless dashes through the mountains, such was her absolute confidence in her chosen champion.

She popped a peppermint lozenge into her mouth and stretched her arms, as carefree as if she were reclining on a divan. 'I'm so glad we have this chance to rendezvous with the old Macnab crew,' she beamed. 'Do you suppose they'll be getting up to more mischief?'

'No such luck,' said Archie. 'The last time I saw any of them, Lamancha was closeted away with the Brazilian ambassador or the Canadian consul or some such, and Leithen was sitting on some deathly dull committee scrutinising export licences. They've settled right back in the old groove like pigeons come home to roost. I doubt they'll do anything more daring than waking the neighbours with a sing-song.'

'Perhaps,' said Janet wistfully, 'we can persuade them to launch a raid on Haripol and make off with Lady Claybody's little dog.'

'I don't regard being stuck with that yapping little blighter as any sort of adventure,' said Archie. 'More of a penance.'

'Perhaps that's what we need,' said the girl, growing unexpectedly serious. 'I know we're lucky to be so blissfully happy, Archie, but in all honesty, we're getting a little too comfortable.'

Archie gritted his teeth, fingers tight on the wheel, as he performed a dizzying swerve around an oncoming horse and cart. The Hispana's outer wheels left the road and spat up a shower of gravel before Archie jerked them back on course.

Janet continued her train of thought, as though oblivious of her husband's hair's breadth manoeuvre. 'Many people strive so hard to gain so little for themselves, I don't feel we have a right to such happiness unless we're prepared to earn it. I think that's a law of the universe and we can't just ignore it.'

Archie couldn't resist chortling at her earnestness. 'I hardly think Leithen and Lamancha are going to dispatch us on a fool's crusade just to satisfy your sense of virtue, old girl.'

'Then maybe it's time we made our own adventures.' Janet tilted her head thoughtfully to one side, then her blue eyes flashed with inspiration. 'I know – what about a trip to South America?'

'South America?' Archie echoed. 'It's liable to be devilishly hot down there, isn't it?'

'The hotter the better,' Janet enthused. 'We could buy ourselves a pair of first class *criollos* and go galloping across the pampas like a couple of gauchos.'

'*Criollos*?' grunted Archie, puzzled.

'South American ponies, silly,' Janet explained. 'They're supposed to be very hardy and quite adorable.'

Archie had been wary of horses since his leg – wounded in the war – had been reinjured in a steeplechase, but he could not resist his wife's radiant zeal.

'Well, it would certainly put me well beyond the reach of even my most troublesome constituents. I say, do you suppose I might get the hang of chucking one of those *bolas* thingies?'

Janet laughed. 'I think if people saw you whirling one of those around your head, they'd be well advised to dive for cover.'

'More chance of me throttling myself actually,' her husband joked.

'Archie, look!' Janet exclaimed suddenly. 'There are two men running down the hill towards us. They're waving frantically, as if they want us to stop.'

Archie looked up with a start of recognition. 'Well, I'll be blowed! It's Lamancha and Palliser-Yeates.'

He pulled up so sharply Janet was jolted out of her seat. Unconcerned, she grabbed the top of the windshield with one hand while using the other to wave a greeting to their friends as they pelted down the slope towards them.

Lamancha jumped onto the running board and doffed his hat to Janet. 'I thought I recognised this car of yours,

Archie. If this isn't a stroke of luck!'

Palliser-Yeates gave the Roylances a merry greeting. 'Just when we're wanting a ride, here you show up, Archie, like a genie out of the bottle.'

'Magic carpet and all,' beamed Janet, patting the Hispana's dashboard.

'So what are you two up to?' Archie asked. 'Has old Leithen sent you off to bag a few rabbits for the pot?'

'Nothing so lighthearted, I'm afraid,' Lamancha replied. 'We're going to need any help you can give us.'

'Are you saying that John Macnab is back in action?' Janet enquired eagerly.

'Yes, he is,' replied Palliser-Yeates, 'and not in any way we could have imagined.'

'We're looking for some missing Germans,' Lamancha explained.

'Germans, you say?' echoed Archie in surprise. 'Well, if it's Germans you want, I know where's there's a whole gang of them.'

11

THE BEASTS OF THE FIELD

———

Once Lamancha and Palliser-Yeates had leapt aboard, Archie turned the Hispana round and made a race of it back to Kinclavers. Not for the first time his friends were grateful that the Hispano-Suiza company was famed for the quality of its brakes. As they sped through the twisting mountain routes, they told the Roylances of Richand Hannay's extraordinary encounter and subsequent events, right up to their discovery of the tell-tale paper fragment.

Archie uttered a low whistle. 'Old Kaiser Bill nobbled right here in our own back yard? Well, that's one for the books all right.'

In spite of his wartime experiences and his new responsibilities as an MP, Archie retained an endearing boyish idiocy which his friends found a refreshing change from the many grave bores they were compelled to mix with in their daily business. They were aware, however, that being tight-lipped had never been his strong point.

'I hope that after a few months in Parliament you've learned the importance of keeping your mouth shut when the occasion calls for it,' said Palliser-Yeates.

'I'll say,' Archie confirmed. 'I put my foot in it once or twice during those first few weeks. Never again. Once bitten and all that.'

'Good,' said Lamancha. 'Maximum discretion is vitally important now.'

'Yes, we understand,' said Janet gravely. 'Right now you only have Duncan Kildennan and his people to deal with. If word got out that the Kaiser was here in Denroy, we might have a whole mob baying for vengeance.'

'Do you suppose somebody could just talk sense to this chap Kildennan?' Archie wondered. 'Dissuade him from whatever drastic steps he has in mind?'

'Well, if anyone can do that, then Leithen and Hannay are the men for the job,' said Palliser-Yeates. 'It's a long shot, though.'

'I've met Kildennan a few times,' said Janet, 'at local fairs and suchlike. He's never slow to tell anyone how much he has sacrificed for this ungrateful country, particularly his two sons, who were well liked hereabouts.'

'Doesn't he have a wife who could bring him round?' asked Archie.

'She died some years ago,' said Janet. 'He has a daughter Christina, who lost a young husband in the war. I hope she's not involved in this business.'

'So who are these Germans you mentioned, Archie?' Lamancha asked.

'Frightful boors, I'm afraid. We'd stopped off at the Kinclavers Hydropathic for a spot of lunch – they do a very tempting lemon sole, you know – and just as we were finishing up, we heard these three chaps kicking up the most awful stink.'

'It looked like the waiter had tripped and spilled soup on one of them,' said Janet. 'He was a big, sullen man, and at first I took his bulk for blubber. When he stood up, though, you could tell it was muscle.'

'He grabbed the waiter by his shirt front and shook him

like a dog,' said Archie. 'Cursed him out in German with a few choice English words thrown in for good measure.'

'A tall man with a head like a cannonball ordered him to settle down,' said Janet. 'Everyone addressed him as "Baron" and he was obviously in charge.'

'Yes,' added Archie. 'He said something like *That's enough, Kurbin. You don't want to kill the little wretch.* Once Kurbin had dropped the waiter, the baron bellowed for the manager, who came running pretty sharply, as you can imagine.'

'Roundhead gave him a horrid earful,' said Janet, 'reminding him that he was a very important guest. You'd have thought he was the king of Siam the way he was carrying on. The poor manager had to grovel like a slave and offer a free lunch for all three before they would let him go.'

'And who was the third man?' Palliser-Yeates asked.

'A little weasel with a ginger moustache,' said Archie. 'He kept his head down during all the fuss. Probably a servant.'

'That's really all we know,' said Janet. 'We were on our way to meet you at the lodge, so we didn't see what happened after. I doubt they're the most popular guests.'

'I know we fought them in the war,' commented Archie, 'but I've always found your average German to be a pretty decent sort of fellow.'

'Not this lot,' said Janet feelingly. 'If anyone round here is up to no good, then I'd bet it's them.'

They crested the top of a hill and saw the handsome stone-built houses of Kinclavers lying below. As they descended they heard the drone of an engine passing overhead. Archie looked up to see a biplane with distinctive red markings descending gracefully as it headed northward over the rooftops.

'I say, that looks like a DH.50!' he exclaimed. 'Those things are brand spanking new. Only somebody with a whacking great wallet could have got his hands on one so soon!'

Lamancha squinted up at the plane. 'There's only one man I can think of who would be flying a crate like that around these parts. Where on earth can he be going?'

'There's a small landing strip just north of here,' said Archie. 'It's only a couple of fields knocked together and flattened out, but it serves.'

He was forced to slow down as they entered the outskirts of the town. In spite of its modest size, Kinclavers was a bustling Highland crossroads for hunters, equestrians, hikers and sightseers. On any given day one might bump into a party of archaeologists investigating the Pictish circles, geologists exploring the volcanic substrata of the mountains, or folklorists seeking the origin of some ancient Gaelic song.

They drove down the bustling main street past hoardings that advertised the latest edition of the *Denroy Weekly Clarion* with the headline *Farm Labour Dispute Worsens*. A trio of high-spirited gents were merrily outfitting themselves at the gun and tackle store, while the local kiltmaker stood in his doorway directing scornful scrutiny at every pair of trousers that passed his shop. Across the street was MacTavish the family butcher, famed for his meat and gravy pies and delicious onion bridies, while next door the window of the bakery was arrayed with currant scones and butteries.

'Look there!' exclaimed Palliser-Yeates, pointing to one

of the other stores. '*Mackie and Son, Purveyors of Fine Food.* I'll bet that's where that wrapping came from.'

'That just confirms that those Germans Archie and Janet spotted are exactly the chaps we're looking for,' said Lamancha.

The town hall clock and the spire of Kinclavers church faced each other across the market square as though engaged in a staring contest between time and eternity. The central fountain had been reduced to a trickle of water that dribbled grudgingly from the mouth of a truculent stone lion whose left ear had been chipped off in the violence of a long ago riot. A shrill whistle and a trailing plume of smoke in the distance announced the passage of a southbound train along the railway track that marked the eastern boundary of the town.

Beyond the square, a disordered flock of sheep had wandered into the street followed by an indolent dog and a furious shepherd, who was swearing loudly that he had only taken his eyes off them for a moment while he partook of some much needed refreshment. Archie muttered some mild imprecations as he tried to force a way through.

'The Hydropathic is just at the end of this road on the left,' said Janet, pointing.

'We'd be there in a few ticks if these wretched animals would just get out of the way,' Archie grumbled.

'Look, Archie, you and Janet get out and leg it up to the hotel,' said Lamancha. 'Keep an eye on those Germans while John and I follow that plane.'

'Of course, if you think it's that urgent,' said Archie agreeably.

He pulled up and he and Janet got out, allowing the other

two men to move into the front seats. As the Roylances worked their way through the sheep to the pavement they heard Lamancha's command ringing behind them.

'Clear the way! Clear the way there!'

As if in response to his unquestionable authority, the woolly mass divided, opening a path for the car as the Red Sea had parted miraculously before Moses. With a lordly wave to the animals, Lamancha proceeded up the road.

'*And God gave him dominion over the beasts of the field,*' murmured Palliser-Yeates, loosely misquoting the Bible.

As they passed beyond the edge of the town Lamancha's sharp eyes fixed intently on the small airfield ahead. 'They've definitely set down there,' he observed.

Palliser-Yeates could see the tension in the set of his friend's jaw. 'Look, Charles, be straight with me – who do you think is in that plane?'

'Unless I'm very much mistaken it's someone who could bring even more trouble down on our heads – Edward Prince of Wales, the heir to the throne.'

Palliser-Yeates uttered a choice exclamation of surprise that was well outside the bounds of his usual language. 'The prince, here at the same time as his cousin the Kaiser? Do you think it's a coincidence?'

'I suppose he could be up here for one of his romantic dalliances,' said Lamancha dubiously, 'but if it is a coincidence, it's a whopper that will take some swallowing.'

'Then it's as we already suspected: old Wilhelm didn't travel all this way just to take in the Highland air.'

'Whatever is going on,' said Lamancha, 'if the Prince of Wales is mixed up in it, then we may be on the brink of a scandal that would rock the nation to its foundations.'

12

PRINCE OF THE SKIES

Once Lamancha had parked the Hispana outside the fence surrounding the airfield, he and Palliser-Yeates entered through a wicket gate. They passed a pair of wooden sheds that had been erected to store fuel and other supplies and saw the plane at the far end of the runway, its engine slowly cooling.

Closer to hand stood a luxurious Rolls-Royce beside which a folding table had been set up by a uniformed chauffeur. He was pouring champagne for the three men who had disembarked from the aircraft, all of whom were evidently in high spirits after their flight. They had just finished a toast when they spotted Lamancha and Palliser-Yeates approaching. Their manner altered immediately from careless celebration to an obvious wariness.

At the centre of the group stood a slight figure who regarded them from beneath his thatch of yellow hair with the wistful face of a choirboy. His innocently youthful aspect contrasted oddly with his garishly patterned tweed suit and his brown and white brogues. Many people regarded the latter as the distinctive footwear of a cad.

Edward Prince of Wales, eldest son of King George V, served in the Grenadier Guards in the war and his frequent visits to the front had made him popular with veterans. Since then, however, his distaste for the normal protocols of royal behaviour – which were particularly expected of the heir to the throne – was proving a matter of grave concern to his father and to the Prime Minister.

The young man's expression was solemn as he assessed the newcomers, then, as though a brilliant light had been switched on, his features were illuminated from within by a glowing smile.

'Lamancha, Charles Lamancha!' he exclaimed jauntily. 'Why, I haven't seen you since the South Oxfordshire Hunt.'

Lamancha shook the offered hand and smiled in return. 'I see, Your Highness, that you're quite recovered from the fall you took.'

The prince laughed lightly. 'Oh, that was nothing. I've taken worse hurt from a broken heart.'

'This is my good friend John Palliser-Yeates.'

The prince acknowledged the introduction with a nod and drained the last of his champagne. As the glass was promptly refilled he indicated the mustachioed figure to his right.

'This is my pilot Flight Lieutenant Eddie Fielden – "Mouse", we call him. The blessed fellow's so timid he wouldn't let me take the wheel of this beauty in case I dented her on her first flight.'

'She takes a bit of handling,' explained the pilot, 'but we'll soon get the kinks out of her.'

On Prince Edward's left stood a very different figure, whose dark probing eyes and assertively outthrust jaw gave a forceful impression of animal vitality combined with an exceptional intelligence.

'This is my friend and financial adviser Warren Creevey,' said the prince. 'Perhaps you've heard of him.'

'Pleased to meet you, Lamancha,' said the noted English financier as they shook hands. 'I hear you're very highly regarded in America, and those people do not impress easily.' His voice was deep and genial and his smile came easily.

'And I believe you're rather a big noise in the City, Mr Creevey,' Lamancha returned.

'Oh, I've pulled off a few coups,' said Creevey, 'but nothing as yet to shake the world.' There was that in his bearing which suggested he was capable of exactly that.

'The way you manipulated those Bolivian stocks caught a few people out,' commented Palliser-Yeates as he and Creevey were introduced.

'It's all about spotting opportunities and seizing them before the other chap wakes up,' said Creevey. 'If we're to get the world back on its feet, we need the proper incentives, and nothing incentivises like money.'

Lamancha was used to sizing men up, but in the case of Creevey he felt as though he were scouting an impregnable fortress in order to assess its defences. The financier had the disarming air of a dreamer, but one whose dreams were an incalculable maze of criss-crossing schemes and sudden, brilliant deceits.

'So, Your Highness, what brings you up here?' asked Lamancha as he and Palliser-Yeates each accepted a freshly poured glass of champagne.

'Sheer boredom, I'm afraid,' the prince declared. 'London has become stiflingly dull, and after suffering through Shaw's new play – some God-awful tosh about a woman atoning to her husband for an affair – well, after that I had to get away and clear my head.'

'Plus we wanted to investigate some new ventures without the royal attendants shadowing us everywhere,' said Creevey.

'Half of those chaps are spies for my father.' Edward shook his head disparagingly. 'I'm glad to be shot of them, frankly.'

Palliser-Yeates took a small sip of champagne. 'Are these ventures something I might invest in?'

'I think they're rather outside your field, if you don't mind my saying so,' Creevey replied, 'and the risks are pretty steep.'

'To hear Creevey talk, you'd think he spent his life wrestling crocodiles and performing dentistry on hungry lions,' joked the prince. 'In fact most of the time he's locked away in secret meetings, spending hours on the phone and shooting off an endless stream of transatlantic telegrams.'

'Don't think that isn't dangerous,' said Creevey with a gleam in his dark, intelligent eyes. 'Some of the most savage beasts on the planet are to be found in the boardroom.'

'I expect Mr Creevey has a few notions that might relieve your boredom,' said Lamancha to the prince.

Edward's laugh was almost melodious. 'Well, he has been pressing me to take a trip to America, haven't you, Creevey? Says I'll find all manner of pleasant company in New York. I believe the clubs there are the last thing in gaiety.'

'That's a flight you'd definitely better let me handle,' Flight Lieutenant Fielden put in.

'Before you take off for the delights of the New World, sir,' said Lamancha, 'might I have a word with you in private?'

'In private?' The prince set his glass aside and raised a comical eyebrow. 'I say, it's not going to be a risqué joke, is it?'

'No, nothing like that,' Lamancha assured him. 'But it is something you will want to hear.'

In spite of a warning glance from Creevey, the prince allowed himself to be drawn away out of earshot, leaving Palliser-Yeates and the financier to discuss the markets while 'Mouse' Fielden did his best to feign interest.

Once he was certain they could not be overheard, Lamancha set about the delicate task of interrogating his future king.

'Look, I think we both know it isn't simply boredom that's brought you all the way to the Highlands. I have to ask you exactly what you're doing here.'

Edward lit a cigarette and took a long draw on it before replying.

'We're meeting some people at a lodge I've rented for the week. I rather fancy a spot of riding, maybe bag a few birds, that sort of thing. Creevey set it all up.' With an airy wave of his cigarette he added, 'I'd invite you along, but I'm afraid it's rather an exclusive group.'

'Might one of those people be a German cousin of yours,' Lamancha probed, 'a man who was once a very important, not to say dangerous, figure in the world?'

Edward's quizzical expression was nearly perfect. 'Honestly, old man, I have no idea what you're talking about.'

Lamancha bit back on his growing impatience with the prince's evasions. He had no doubt that his hunch was correct and that the only course open to him was to lay his cards plainly on the table.

'I happen to know that Wilhelm von Hohenzollern is right here in Scotland, possibly only a few miles away,' he said.

Edward flicked some ash to the ground and responded peevishly. 'Really? That sounds unlikely, doesn't it? And if it were true, then it's a family matter and none of your business.'

'When I see a fuse burning on a bloody great keg of gunpowder, I think it's my business to snuff it out,' Lamancha told him sharply. 'What would people think of you if they knew you were meeting with the most hated man in Europe?'

An edge of anger flashed beneath Edward's boyish charm. 'A lot of people would think it's a jolly good idea. You see what's happening over there, plots, murders and Bolshies running around all over trying to bring the world crashing down about our ears.'

'And your friend Creevey has the solution, does he?' Lamancha was as sceptical as good manners would allow.

Edward cast an uneasy glance in the financier's direction, as if afraid he might hear. 'Last year Creevey was hobnobbing with that German Stinnes and a few other bigwigs. They came up with the notion of certain interested parties getting together in secret to discuss the future of Germany.'

'They think they can restore the old order?'

'There's a new movement afoot,' said the prince, suddenly heated, 'one that will bring its own order. We can either play our part or let it all go to the devil.'

'I'm afraid your little conference has already fallen apart,' Lamancha informed him grimly. 'Wilhelm has been kidnapped by a man named Kildennan.'

Edward blanched visibly. 'You mean old Duncan Kildennan, the laird?'

'Yes. I don't think he's taken him home for tea. He has something a lot less pleasant in mind.'

The prince's mouth twisted into a hint of scorn. 'How on earth do you know all this? Crystal ball?'

'I don't have time to tell you the whole story,' Lamancha answered curtly. 'My friends Dick Hannay and Ned Leithen have gone off to prise Wilhelm out of Kildennan's clutches, but there's every chance this will all end very badly.'

Edward tossed away his half finished cigarette and began edging back towards the Rolls. 'Look, Lamancha, I know you're a sound fellow and I'm sure you mean well, but you really are poking your nose in where it's not wanted.'

Lamancha resisted the impulse to grab hold of the prince to keep him in place. 'You must get away from here as soon as possible. If you sink any further into this mess, the throne itself might be in danger.'

Edward turned away and walked briskly back to Creevey's side. The financier's eyes darted between the prince and Lamancha. 'Important business, was it?' he enquired sharply.

'Not at all,' answered Edward, forcing a laugh. 'Lamancha was just offering me a few tips for the next race at Aintree. Got them right from the horse's mouth so to speak.'

'Perhaps we'd better be on our way,' suggested Creevey, motioning to the chauffeur to clear away the drinks.

'Yes, sorry we can't carry on our chat,' said Edward, dismissing Lamancha and Palliser-Yeates. 'I'm sure you've got things to be getting on with.'

With a perfunctory bow, Lamancha turned and led his friend away.

'So, is the prince connected to this business?' Palliser-Yeates asked as they returned to the Hispana.

'He's right in the thick of it,' Lamancha answered grimly. 'I only hope he'll take my advice and get clear while there's still time.'

13

JANET MACNAB

The Kinclavers Hydropathic was a product of the nineteenth-century craze for 'water cures'. In her eagerness to find a remedy for gout, rheumatism and over-consumption, Scotland heartily embraced the new science of medical bathing, simplified diet and the regular consumption of foul-tasting mineral water.

The hotel occupied a generous spread of high ground a quarter of a mile to the west of the town, a handsome neo-baronial edifice four floors high, with a crow-stepped roof and a matched pair of pepperpot turrets at either end. The ground and first floors were furnished with verandas to provide sheltered access to fresh air and natural light in all weathers, while its frontage boasted a terraced lawn equipped with folding chairs and umbrellas.

Though the Hydropathic's origins were medical, enthusiasm for the benefits of balneology was already on the wane when it was commandeered as a military hospital during the Great War. When it was returned to civilian use, this merely accelerated the process of catering to a much wider range of guests, many of whom had no desire to 'take the waters', but merely sought rest and relaxation amid scenic Highland surroundings.

As the Roylances made their way up the drive, past regimented ranks of copper beeches, Janet wondered out loud, 'Archie, why is Charles so concerned about that plane? Who do you think is aboard?'

Archie shrugged. 'Maybe one of his colleagues in the cabinet. It's a four-seater, so maybe a whole gang of them.' An unpleasant thought suddenly struck him with such force that he gave himself a light smack on the forehead. 'I say, I hope it's not the Prime Minister. I'm supposed to be on my way back to London by now, not dawdling about here.'

Passing through the glassy double doors, they entered a foyer decorated in restful shades of rose and pale green, where paintings of tame waterfalls and wild geese in flight added to the pastoral atmosphere. A scattering of wicker chairs and a minor forest of potted palms were intended to give the impression of a tropical paradise transplanted to the harsher landscape of Wester Ross. Somewhere a piano tinkled brightly and a placard announced there was to be a musical soiree that evening featuring extracts from Mendelssohn's Scottish Symphony.

Archie and Janet scouted the lounges, library and sitting rooms that spread across the ground floor until they spotted the baron seated at a table beneath a portrait of Bonnie Prince Charlie. With him were the weasel with the ginger moustache and a sallow-skinned man with an oriental cast to his features. There was no sign of the heavy-set Kurbin who had given the waiter such a hard time earlier in the day. The baron was drinking gin and bitters while his minions were restricted to coffee.

The Roylances seated themselves casually at the nearest empty table and feigned interest in the papers and magazines heaped there. The Germans were talking freely in their own tongue, confident that no one in this part of the world would be able to understand them.

Archie cocked an ear and frowned. 'I've got a smattering of the lingo but they're talking so fast I might easily get the wrong end of the stick.'

Janet put a finger to his lips to silence him. 'My sister and I have had a pretty comprehensive education in German,' she whispered. 'My Aunt Isobel insisted that you couldn't call yourself civilised until you'd read Goethe.'

Archie beamed. 'You never cease to amaze me, you wondrous woman.'

Janet cast a sidelong glance at the three foreigners. 'Pretend you're talking to me, Archie, but keep your voice low so I can listen in on our friends.'

Archie picked up a copy of the local paper and reported the farming news to his wife in a muted murmur. Janet smiled and nodded but kept her ear attuned to the Germans. Archie saw her eyes widen. She bit her lip and clutched at her skirt as she took in the full import of what they were saying.

She stood up abruptly. Catching Archie by the arm, she pulled him to his feet and drew him over to a quiet corner of the foyer.

'They do have a prisoner upstairs,' she told him, 'somebody called Ilsemann. That beast Kurbin is standing guard over him and now they're discussing the best method of doing away with him. They plan to drug him and roll him out in one of the hydro's wheelchairs.'

'And he won't be making a return trip, eh?' Archie clenched his fist. 'I'd like to give those swine a good thrashing.'

'We need to get that poor chap out of here before they

go to fetch him.' A gleam of excitement flashed in Janet's blue eyes. 'It's time for us to step into John Macnab's shoes and do a spot of poaching.'

'It won't be easy,' said Archie, glancing back to where the Germans were seated. 'They're a pretty tough-looking crew.'

'Look, I've got an idea,' said Janet. 'You find out what rooms they're in. I'll be back in a minute.'

She disappeared into one of the hotel's back passages while Archie ambled over to the well-groomed young clerk manning the front desk. Adopting his most disarming manner, he said, 'I wonder if you could help me. There's a German gentleman I met at lunch here. He invited me to join him in his room later for some buttered crumpets.'

'Yes, that would be Baron von Hilderling and his party,' said the clerk with a grimace. 'We're all well aware of his presence.'

'Well, the thing is,' Archie continued, 'I'm blessed if I can remember the room number. I think it's something like 501.'

The clerk opened the register and ran a finger down the page with a snort of distaste. 'Buttered crumpets, you say?'

'Yes, the chap's simply mad for them.'

'The baron and his party are in rooms 321 and 322,' said the clerk, then added in a warning tone, 'if you're absolutely sure you want to join them.'

'Thanks ever so much,' said Archie, strolling away. 'I'm such an ass not to have remembered.'

He ducked down a passage out of sight of the desk and met Janet on her way back from the staff quarters. She had borrowed an apron and lace cap and at first glance looked every inch the hotel maid.

Archie appraised her disguise with an admiring smile. '321 and 322,' he told her.

'Good,' said Janet, plucking a fire extinguisher from its niche in the wall. 'Grab hold of that fire bucket there and follow me.'

Archie seized the handle of the red bucket of sand and marched up the stairs after his wife. As they ascended she explained her plan.

Once on the third floor, Archie concealed himself behind a large rubber plant while Janet knocked loudly on the door of room 322. When there was no response she switched to 321 and rapped insistently until the door opened and Kurbin's angry face peered out.

His bulk loomed large, blocking any view of the room beyond. 'I do not wish to be disturbed,' he growled.

'Quick, sir, quick!' Janet panted with breathless urgency. 'You must follow me! There's a fire and the hotel is being evacuated!'

Kurbin stuck his head out into the passage and sniffed. 'I smell no smoke. I hear nothing. Go away!'

Before he could disappear behind the door Janet slammed the base of the fire extinguisher down hard on his right foot, throwing all her weight behind it for maximum force. Kurbin crumpled up with a howl of pain and a vicious curse that Janet's German tuition had overlooked.

Before the man could recover, Archie stepped out of hiding and hurled the contents of the fire bucket into his face. As the German clawed blindly at the sand in his eyes, Archie swung the empty bucket at his head and connected with a loud clang. The impact knocked the big man backwards into the room and laid him out flat on the carpet.

Archie and Janet darted inside, slamming the door shut behind them. While her husband pinned down the stunned Kurbin, Janet hurried to where Ilsemann lay on the bed, bound and gagged. Years of camping and boating had given her a facility with knots and she had him untied in a matter of seconds.

He stirred groggily and from the glazed look in his eyes she could tell he was fighting off the effects of a drug. She plucked a pitcher from a nearby table and flung the water full in his face.

'Wake up!' she urged. 'We have to get out of here!'

Ilsemann nodded feebly and wiped his face with his sleeve.

Sprawled on the floor, Kurbin let out a groan and Archie clamped a hand over his mouth. 'Let's get this chap tied up before he comes to.'

They transferred the ropes to Kurbin and stuffed the discarded gag into his mouth. 'Just like trussing up a turkey,' Janet panted as she secured the last knot.

Archie helped Ilsemann to his feet. 'Come on, old chap, we need to make tracks.'

Janet flung open the door and led the way out. Two steps beyond the threshold they fetched up short at the sound of German voices coming from the main staircase.

Janet turned to her husband. 'Get him out the back way,' she ordered, pushing the two men in the other direction. 'I'll stall them somehow.'

Her tone brooked no argument. With a nod Archie bundled Ilsemann towards a bend in the passage. The instant they were out of sight, Janet hurried to the head of the stairs to confront Baron von Hilderling and his two minions before they could reach the upper floor.

'I'm sorry, sir, you have to go back!' she announced loudly, raising her hands in front of the baron, who was in the lead. 'There's a fire!'

An expression of arrogant vexation contorted Hilderling's features. 'Get out of the way!' he roared, trying to push past her.

'I'm afraid I really must insist,' said Janet, and threw herself at his chest.

Her charge caught the baron completely off guard. With an outraged bellow, he staggered backwards, toppling into the arms of his two companions. All three went tumbling down the stairs to end up in a bruised heap on the landing below.

Janet bounded down the steps and leapt over the groaning Germans with the grace of a gazelle. When she reached the ground floor she raced to the dinner gong and began hammering it furiously.

'Fire! Fire!' she yelled. 'Get everyone out of the building!'

The cry was taken up by staff and guests up and down the hotel. When Hilderling and his men got to their feet they were met by other guests rushing down the stairs who insisted the three Germans join them in following the proper fire drill. While that struggle was going on, the hotel manager appeared and snatched the hammer from Janet's hand before she could strike the gong again.

'What in heaven's name are you doing?' he demanded, red-faced with outrage. He had to raise his voice above the hubbub of confusion that now filled the building. 'You're not one of my staff!'

'Aren't I?' Janet responded innocently. 'I'm most frightfully sorry. I must have stumbled into the wrong hotel.'

The manager suddenly found himself surrounded by irate guests demanding to know whether this was a real fire or just some damned fool drill. Leaving him to babble back at them in utter perplexity, Janet discarded the borrowed cap and apron and made for the exit.

14

THE REVEREND ARCHIE

Archie and the freed captive went barrelling down the back stairway at breakneck speed. Still unsteady on his feet, the young German would have taken a tumble if his rescuer hadn't gripped him by the shoulder.

Beyond the foot of the stairs lay a whitewashed passageway giving access to the service areas of the hotel. There was no one about, the staff having evidently obeyed Janet's fire alarm.

'Now to find a way out,' said Archie.

They moved swiftly along the passage and through a door at the far end. This took them into a spacious laundry furnished with two large copper boilers, a double row of washtubs and an array of ironing tables. They exited by a set of double doors that opened onto a drying green at the rear of the hotel.

Archie pulled up and grabbed his leg with a grunt of pain. 'Old war wound,' he apologised. 'Never mind, though. I'll be fine.'

While they paused to take their bearings, Ilsemann said, 'I am grateful to you, but I have an *associate* who is also in difficulties.'

'Oh, you mean old Wilhelm,' said Archie.

Ilsemann started. 'So you know?'

'Well, I confess to being a bit vague on the details,' said Archie, 'but I know that while the two of you were wandering about Denroy the old Kaiser was bagged by a local laird.'

The young German clutched Archie's arm urgently. 'Yes, he has been betrayed, and the danger is most pressing.'

'I shouldn't worry too much,' Archie assured him. 'Some friends of mine have gone to fetch him. Our priority right now is to get shot of those ugly customers back there.'

They made their way round to the front of the building where a sizeable crowd was milling about on the terrace. Keeping their heads low, they slipped away from the hotel and headed towards the gates.

'How many people know?' Ilsemann enquired as they strode briskly down the drive.

'About Wilhelm? Only a few, and we need to keep it that way,' said Archie, 'otherwise we're liable to stir up a hornet's nest of trouble. I say, what do I call you?'

'I am Captain Sigurd von Ilsemann, adjutant to His Majesty the Kaiser,' the young officer replied with automatic formality.

'Pleased to meet you, Siggy. I'm Archie Roylance. Believe it or not I'm the local MP, though I've certainly never gone to this much trouble for any of my constituents. Just as well nobody ever recognises me.'

At the bottom of the drive they struck the main road into town. As they crossed over and made for the cover of the stone-built houses, Ilsemann glanced back.

'*Ach, du Schreck!*' he exclaimed.

Archie wheeled about and saw the baron emerge from behind the beech trees with Kurbin and his other two servants. At the sight of his prey Hilderling pulled a pistol from his pocket, but realised immediately that there were too many witnesses about. Stuffing the gun back out of sight, he redoubled his pace.

Limping badly now, Archie led the way down a narrow side street. Eyes peeled for a hiding place, they swerved round a woman with a pram and an old man walking his dog.

'I warn you, my friend,' said Ilsemann, 'that von Hilderling will not hold back from any action, however disgraceful.'

'Under normal circumstances,' said Archie ruefully, 'I'd find the local bobby, but we need to keep you under wraps.' Suddenly he spotted an open doorway leading into the rear of a large civic hall. 'Come on, we'll duck in there.'

Darting inside, they found themselves in a long, ill-lit passageway where two figures immediately blocked their way. One was a large, fat man in a bowler hat, the other looked old enough to have made the personal acquaintance of John Knox.

'I'm sorry, gentlemen, but this is a private meeting,' the stout fellow informed them loftily.

Archie knew the baron was close enough to have spotted them ducking into the building and any delay might allow him to catch up. 'But I swear we were invited,' he improvised. 'You simply have to let us in.'

'Invited?' echoed the old man. 'Oh, it will be yourself then? When we heard about the train derailment at Abermoil we were afraid you wouldn't make it.'

Archie was taken aback. 'Myself?' he faltered, then pulled himself manfully together. 'Absolutely.'

The old man clucked his tongue. 'What I mean to say is, you'll be the Reverend Murdo Abercrombie – from the Free Eden Church?'

Archie's voice failed him and he nodded automatically.

A broad smile spread across the ancient's withered features. He seized Archie by the hand and pumped it enthusiastically. 'It is a great honour to meet you, sir, a great honour. Though I am surprised to find you such a young man.'

Archie groped for a suitable rejoinder. 'Oh, I take care of myself,' he managed. 'Plenty of vegetables and lots of exercise, you know.' He mimed hoisting a set of barbells up and down.

'It's the clean living that does it, I'm sure,' the old man agreed, 'a strict regimen of prayer and the Bible. And your friend would be . . . ?'

'My friend?' Archie echoed, turning to Ilsemann. The German had the lost look of a man cast completely adrift on some alien sea. 'Oh, yes, this is my associate and . . . um . . . chief chorister, the Reverend . . . er . . .'

At this point Archie's invention gave out and he had to ransack his memory for the name of an old school chum. What popped into his head was a small, red-headed ruffian who had once flattened him on the rugby field. 'The Reverend Tarquin Muldoon.'

The old man raised a bushy eyebrow in horror. 'Muldoon, d'ye say? That sounds like an *Irish* name.'

'Does it?' Archie responded lamely. 'I can't say I've ever thought about it.'

'Aye, well, we'll let that pass for the present,' the ancient conceded. 'He has no doubt purged himself of the errors of his benighted ancestors.'

'Oh, he has,' Archie assured him. 'Like a dose of salts.'

Ilsemann forced an uneasy smile of agreement at this unexpected assessment of his character.

'This way, gentlemen, this way,' said their host, leading them down the passage. 'Everything is ready.'

Behind them a disturbance at the door announced the arrival of the baron and his men. Archie braced himself for flight but was gratified to hear the fat man trenchantly refusing them entry.

He became aware that the old man was speaking to him. 'I am Pastor James Swivelling,' he said with a deferential bow. 'You have heard of me, perhaps, even in far-off Stornoway?'

'Indeed, indeed,' Archie affirmed. 'The name of Pastor James Swellinghurst is never far from my lips.'

'Swivelling,' the ancient corrected him.

'Exactly, just as you say.'

'There's quite a crowd, all eager to hear you speak, Mr Abercrombie. Will Mr Muldoon be saying a few words also?'

'No, no, he's more a man of prayer,' Archie demurred. 'Silent prayer.'

He threw a glance at Ilsemann who responded with a severe nod, showing he was well aware that his accent would blow the whole game.

They were led up onto a stage where two other bearded dignitaries were already seated. They muttered a greeting and beckoned to the newcomers to sit down.

To his alarm, Archie saw that the hall before them was crammed with nearly two hundred people on fold-out canvas chairs. They were mostly men of all ages, with a handful of women being restricted to one far corner. There were perhaps half a dozen children among them, all in various stages of discontent.

The arrival of the visitors sent a buzz of anticipation through the audience. Swivelling silenced them with an upraised hand as he took up position behind a small table set out with a pitcher of water and two glasses.

'It is a great and legitimate pleasure,' he announced, 'to welcome here today one of the champions of the pure Christian faith, unadulterated by the accretions of prideful prelates and muddle-minded moderns.'

This bold alliteration was greeted by an outburst of unseemly cheers which Swivelling quelled with a frown as condemnatory as the Book of Jeremiah.

'He has valiantly opposed those who would place good deeds above faith,' he continued, 'and exalt Latin, the speech of a pagan people, above the honest Scots tongue. I am sure many of you have read his stringently reasoned pamphlets: *The Curse of Babylonian Idolatry*, *A Return to the Pure Edenic Principles*, and *The Seven Errors of Hebraism*.'

He paused to survey his audience with a piercing eye, assuring himself that they fully grasped the gravity and significance of the occasion. He noted with approval the stern expressions on the faces of the men and the noble efforts of the women to suppress the fidgeting of their bored offspring.

'He is a man grounded in true Christian virtue, a savage upholder of the Sabbath, and a relentless foe of episcopal corruption. He is wise, eloquent, and above all *biblical*.' The last word was uttered with an almost ecstatic relish. 'Gentlemen and ladies, I present to you that tireless defender of fundamental Christian truth, the Reverend Murdo Abercrombie.'

Everyone in the room clapped, though the applause was muted by a becoming respect, as suited so sombre a gathering.

At an encouraging gesture from his host, Archie slowly rose to his feet, appalled at the realisation that he was expected to deliver a sermon. Archie's relationship with the Almighty was similar to that he shared with many of his more distant friends. They met for special occasions such as weddings and funerals, found themselves broadly in agreement about most matters, and parted amicably until next time. Neither made any unreasonable demands of the other. While he regularly extolled the benignity of Divine Providence for uniting him with his beloved Janet, he felt more than a little unequal to the task of expounding upon the deeper thoughts and future intentions of his Creator.

Once the clapping had subsided, Archie experienced a twinge of panic as he gazed out over an expanse of terrifyingly expectant faces with no prospect of escape. He recalled from Sunday school that, after his resurrection, the Lord Jesus was able to walk through walls and disappear at will. Never in all his life had he been so envious of his Saviour.

He had in his time delivered one or two political speeches, but those had the benefit of some preparation, however shoddy. Chaps like Charles Lamancha, he knew, could whip up a piece of improvised oratory on almost any subject without prior warning, but this was a gift that had been denied him. His brief acquaintance with the practice of statecraft had, however, taught him a few lessons in the art of stalling for time.

He picked up the water pitcher and slowly – ever so slowly – filled one of the glasses. He then raised the glass to his lips with a stately reverence that bought him a few more precious seconds while he cudgelled his brain for inspiration. After three long, drawn-out sips, he set the glass down and cleared his throat.

'Fellow brethren – and ladies – as I look out upon your faces today,' he began, 'I am reminded of a field of lilies which neither sow nor reap and yet are pleasing to the Lord. I don't mean to say that you're lazy. No, I'm sure you all work very hard, but you are not vain like the bees of the field, which, I expect, buzz around the lilies rather annoyingly.'

He was heartened by a loud grunt of approval from a nonagenarian in the front row who was struggling to adjust his ear trumpet.

'As I look out upon your honest, welcoming faces, I am reminded of the wise words of the prophet Hezekiah, when he spoke of . . .' Here he faltered and was compelled to refill his glass to take two more swallows of water.

'Spoke of matters that concern all of us on an almost daily basis,' he resumed at last. 'Yes, his words on that subject were both wise and profound, and I'm sure you can recall them quite clearly without any prompting from me. If the prophet were here today, I have absolutely no doubt that he would use those exact same words, and I therefore feel no need to repeat them, certain as I am that they are already familiar to you.'

With his confidence growing, Archie began to wag an admonitory finger at his listeners.

'Did not the prophet say that whosoever throws a stone at his brother will break the glass of the tabernacle, and what a terrible mess that will make? And let us not forget about charity, for it is not blown up nor does it trumpet its own noise all over the place. No, charity is like a mushroom seed that grows in a dark place and is then harvested a hundredfold – along with some fish.'

'And what of the whore of Babylon?' one of the righteous interjected. 'Will she be cast down?'

The allusion was lost on Archie but he persevered. 'I imagine she's in for a perfectly frightful time, what with pitchforks and hot coals, the full brimstone. I certainly wouldn't want to be in her shoes.'

As he smiled appreciatively at the widespread murmurs of agreement, Archie saw the door at the back of the hall open silently. Baron von Hilderling and Kurbin slipped in unobtrusively and took up positions against the wall. The baron's right hand was in his pocket, no doubt gripping his pistol. Archie guessed that the other two Germans would be guarding the rear entrance. He and Ilsemann were completely penned in.

15

FOXES AND HOUNDS

Archie threw a glance back at Ilsemann. It was clear from his furrowed brow that he too had noted the presence of the enemy. All Archie could think of to do was to keep talking and play for time.

In the brief gap of silence one of the younger members of the congregation was unable to contain his fervour. Leaping to his feet, he shook a vengeful fist and demanded, 'And when will punishment be delivered unto the unjust?'

Several others loudly reiterated this question, pressing the speaker for an answer.

'I shouldn't worry about that,' Archie assured them. 'I have it on good authority that any day now the unjust will be getting it in the neck. In fact, I believe that a jolly hot furnace is being stoked up just for them, never mind about the price of coal.'

This statement of intent was greeted with raucous approval.

'And the wicked shall feel the Lord's displeasure!' one woman exclaimed in an overflow of spiritual zeal.

'There's no doubt of that,' Archie affirmed, warming to his subject. 'Yes, there will be much smiting of the wicked and all manner of beasts will be numbered. It wouldn't surprise me in the least if the lion should beget with the ram and crow three times before noon. On that day I fully expect the sun to stand still in the sky, as it did when Ahab shook the gates of Nineveh.'

There was a palpable excitement animating the crowd now. Even if they couldn't grasp the exact sense of Archie's words, the increasingly forthright tone of them was very much to their liking. As he fixed his eyes on Hilderling and Kurbin, a sudden inspiration struck him and he threw caution to the winds.

'And what if the unrighteous should come into our very midst?' he challenged his listeners. 'What if they should trespass upon the very nave of the temple? Should we not smite them?'

'Aye, we should!' affirmed several bold voices, almost cracking with emotion.

'They may have stepped through that very door,' Archie declaimed, pointing towards the back of the hall, 'but they shall not pass through the eye of a camel!'

All heads turned to behold the strangers who had entered hitherto unnoticed. Faced with the accusing eyes of the righteous, the two Germans gave a guilty start that brought a thundercloud of condemnation down on them.

'He shall not suffer an unrighteous man!' shrieked a black-clad beanpole of a fellow, trembling with indignation.

'I should jolly well say he won't,' Archie agreed. 'And neither should we if we're worth our salt.'

Baron von Hilderling had faced many dangers in his time, but none was so daunting as this mob of zealous Presbyterians, rising to their feet as one, their faces ablaze with a fanaticism that had not been seen in Scotland since the days of the Covenanters. The baron blanched and threw open the door. He and Kurbin made a swift exit before violent hands could be laid upon them.

Archie stepped around the table to stand on the very edge of the stage. For a moment he felt possessed by the spirit of the Duke of Wellington ordering the victorious advance at Waterloo. 'Brothers and sisters,' he intoned, 'let us take to the streets and there proclaim the justice of the Lord!'

With a huge cheer the crowd surged to the back of the hall, toppling their chairs as they went. As they pressed through the narrow door two abreast, Archie hauled Ilsemann to his feet and led him down into the midst of the mob.

'Come on, Siggy. With this escort I think we can make it safely outside.'

The young captain shook his head admiringly. 'Mr Roylance, you are an extraordinary man.'

'So my wife tells me,' Archie beamed, 'though up until now I wouldn't have believed it myself.'

In the midst of the crowd, they were carried along like a boat swept on by a tidal surge. By the time they reached the high street the whole congregation was singing an ancient hymn filled with fire, blood and martial resolve. Many of them brandished well-thumbed Bibles as though they were flaming torches. Innocent bystanders shrank back into the nearest doorways and gaped awestruck at the sight of the Kirk Militant on the march.

Archie gazed about in wonderment at what he had accomplished. 'You know, I think I could make a fair stab at this preaching lark. Perhaps I missed my calling.'

In spite of their escape Ilsemann was clearly anxious, though not for himself. 'You must take me to the Kaiser,' he insisted. 'He needs me.'

'All in good time, old boy,' Archie responded, 'all in good time. Everything's well in hand.'

'Archie! Archie!' a familiar and beloved voice called out over the bellicose din of the hymns.

Archie searched this way and that until he spotted the fading sunlight glinting off Janet's golden hair as she hopped up and down to make herself visible over the heads of the crowd. He answered her frantic waves and forced his way through the crowd towards her with Ilsemann following in his wake.

Janet grabbed his hand and treated him to an enthusiastic peck on the cheek. 'Oh, Archie, I knew you'd get away. But what on earth is going on? It's like a second Reformation.'

'I hope it won't come to that,' said Archie with feeling. 'With any luck they'll calm down after a while. Janet, this is Captain von Ilsemann. Siggy, this is my wife Janet.'

'Many thanks for your assistance, madam,' Ilsemann responded with a bow. 'I owe you both my very life.'

'This way!' Janet bounded off down a cobbled street. 'I spotted Charles and John driving back into town and managed to flag them down. I've filled them in on what happened at the hotel.'

The Hispana was parked outside a bookshop in the shade of a spreading chestnut tree. Lamancha and Palliser-Yeates, who were leaning against the car, snapped to attention when they saw the rest of the party approaching.

'You'll never guess who was in that plane,' Janet told Archie. 'It was the Prince of Wales.'

Archie goggled at her. 'What, Prince Edward? Well, that's a turn-up for the books!'

Lamancha thumped a fist on the car's bonnet. 'He's a damned fool for getting himself mixed up in this business.'

'It is all part of Baron von Hilderling's plan,' Ilsemann explained when Archie had introduced him to the two Macnabs. 'Thanks to the goodwill already generated by Hugo Stinnes and others, he was able to set up this secret conclave. He used Prince Edward's written guarantee to convince the emperor it was safe to come here.'

'Not so safe after all, as it turns out,' said Palliser-Yeates.

'That was the baron's intent all along,' said Ilsemann. 'He wants the death of the Kaiser to provoke an international crisis his allies in Germany can twist to their own ends.'

'Speaking of the baron,' said Janet, 'we'd better get out of here before he catches up with us.'

'The lady is correct,' Ilsemann agreed. 'We must hasten to the assistance of the emperor.'

Lamancha had moved to the driver's door but Archie nudged him gently aside. 'You'd best let me take the wheel, Charles.'

'If you're quite sure . . .' Lamancha conceded reluctantly.

Janet flung herself into the front passenger seat beside Archie while the other three climbed into the back. The engine started with a roar and they slipped around the outskirts of town to avoid the evangelical throng occupying the high street.

'We'll be at Rushforth Lodge by nightfall,' Archie promised as they sped down the southbound road.

Ilsemann was becoming increasingly agitated. 'Gentlemen, I must impress upon you the absolute urgency of finding the emperor.'

'We're well aware of that,' said Palliser-Yeates.

'Rest assured, captain,' Lamancha added, 'that two of our best men, Edward Leithen and Richard Hannay, set out to snatch him from the clutches of this Kildennan.'

'I'd bet a packet on those two,' said Archie. 'They've gotten out of stickier scrapes.'

'But suppose there's no word from them?' Janet asked.

'We had agreed to rendezvous at a place called Castle Crachan,' said Palliser-Yeates. 'Do you know it?'

'Yes, on the shore of Loch Dhuie,' said Janet. 'I used to go camping there with my cousins.'

Ilsemann's fingers tensed around the door handle. 'We must go there at once.'

'There's no sense in stumbling about in the dark,' cautioned Lamancha. 'We'll catch a few hours' sleep at the lodge and if Dick and Ned haven't turned up by morning, we'll set out to find them.'

To their right the sun was already setting behind the pine-clad Denroy hills while to the left an expanse of heather-covered hillocks rolled away like waves on a purple sea. With so many bends in the road, even Archie had to slow occasionally as the light faded. They were accelerating down a straight stretch when Palliser-Yeates looked back and saw a green Daimler closing from behind. The fact that it was moving rapidly enough to catch up with them sounded an immediate alarm.

'I've got an ugly feeling we've picked up some company,' he growled.

The words were no sooner out of his mouth than two gunshots rang out over the noise of the Hispana's engine.

16

A PRIVATE LITTLE WAR

Lamancha darted a hawk-like glare at their pursuers. 'Well, captain, it looks as though your friend von Hilderling has picked up our trail.'

'He's a determined sort of chap, isn't he?' Archie remarked as they jolted over a bump in the road.

'He knows I can reveal that it was the emperor's own countrymen who betrayed him,' said Ilsemann. 'He cannot let me live if his damnable plan is to succeed.'

A series of corkscrew bends loomed before them. Whipping the wheel this way and that, Archie was aware that the road itself was giving their enemies a chance to fire a broadside. Shots rang out, peppering the left-hand side of the Hispana's chassis. Stubbornly setting his jaw, Archie bore down harder on the throttle.

For the first time in their short marriage Janet felt it necessary to caution her husband. 'Don't let us go crashing off the road, Archie. We'll be sitting ducks if we do.'

'No fear of that,' said Archie through gritted teeth. 'Those bounders are determined to risk all to catch us, though.'

Palliser-Yeates gave a frustrated groan. 'If we could only get our rifles out of the boot.'

The situation triggered Lamancha's instinct for command. He said crisply, 'Archie, if you can get us just one minute's lead on them, John and I will bundle out, grab the guns and hold them off while the rest of you carry on to Rushforth Lodge.'

Archie flashed a grin over his shoulder. 'I reckon I can pull that off, if you're ready for a few risky moves.'

'But that will leave just the two of you against four of them,' Janet objected.

'Don't you worry about us,' Lamancha told her. 'Your job is to get Captain von Ilsemann and his Kaiser to safety. If we don't show up, you must rendezvous with Hannay and Leithen at Castle Crachan.'

'Yes, don't worry about us,' Palliser-Yeates added with slightly less confidence.

Playing fast and loose with the confines of the road, Archie skewed dangerously left and right to short-cut the curves. Through his usual combination of skill and foolhardiness he was able to draw them briefly out of sight of their pursuers behind a sharp granite crag.

'Right, here!' snapped Lamancha.

Archie slammed on the brakes, flinging everyone forward with a wrench. Lamancha and Palliser-Yeates tumbled out of the back. They threw open the boot and grabbed their rifles along with a box of spare ammunition. Lamancha slammed the boot down and gave it a slap, as though sending a skittish horse on its way.

The car roared off as Lamancha and Palliser-Yeates vaulted into shelter behind some boulders. They rested their guns on the rocks and sighted down their barrels at the road, fixing their aim through the twilight. They could hear the approaching engine only seconds away now.

'We'll shoot out their tyres,' said Lamancha. 'I'll take the front, you the back.'

'It will have to be a quick shot.' Palliser-Yeates squinted down the barrel of his rifle. 'They're flying along at the devil's own pace.'

The Daimler hurtled into view with Kurbin hunched over the wheel like an angry ogre. One man leaned out of the passenger side, another from the rear, each with a pistol poised for a sight of their prey.

Lamancha and Palliser-Yeates fired as one. Two tyres burst and the car veered wildly. As the driver fought for control the Macnabs had time to loose off another volley before the vehicle crashed sidelong into a rocky outcrop on the far side of the road.

Palliser-Yeates gave a crow of satisfaction. 'What now, Charles?'

'We need to make sure they can't get their car started. We'll pin them down until Archie's well clear.'

They could hear the voice of Baron von Hilderling screeching angry commands. Bruised and shaken, his men responded as instinctively as beasts to a lash. They crawled out onto the ground and, using the car for cover, began firing randomly at the darkening hillside on the opposite side of the road.

Finally the baron ordered them to cease the futile waste of ammunition and a sudden silence descended. After a full minute's pause, Kurbin came crawling around the front of the Daimler.

'It looks as though that fellow's being sent to find out if we've sneaked off,' Palliser-Yeates observed.

'Let's tell him to mind his own business,' murmured Lamancha.

He fired two warning shots that punched a pair of

holes in the car's radiator. As fluid spouted out over the ground, Kurbin scrambled back into cover.

Now that they had revealed their position, the Macnabs crouched low while a volley of pistol shots knocked chips from their protective boulders. Once the firing had died down again, Palliser-Yeates risked a cautious peek at the enemy position.

'What do you think, Charles?' he breathed. 'Will they try to rush us?'

Lamancha considered the tactical options as he reloaded. 'They might wait until the cover of dark gives them the opportunity to outflank us. On the other hand . . .'

Even as he spoke, they spotted one of the Germans crawling out of the heather about ten yards to their left and trying to slither unseen across the road. Palliser-Yeates loosed off a shot that almost nipped one of his fingers and sent him scurrying back to his companions.

'Look, I know they're Boche and villains to boot,' the banker said, 'but I don't want to be explaining any dead Germans to the local police.'

'No, that would be awkward,' Lamancha agreed. He gestured towards the pine-covered hillside at their back. 'As soon as we get the chance we should make a run for the trees. I doubt they'd be able to catch up with us in the dark.'

As though they had overheard their enemy's intent, the baron and his men began peppering the hillside with bullets.

'I think they're pinning us down for an assault,' Palliser-Yeates surmised grimly.

'Well, if they're determined to back us into a corner,' said Lamancha, 'we'll just have to fight it out and hang the consequences.'

At that moment a shot boomed directly behind them. Both men swung round in a defensive crouch and beheld the last thing they would have expected.

Emerging from the treeline was a young officer sporting a lieutenant's insignia and wearing a Balmoral bonnet with a regimental stag's head badge. His discharged pistol was pointed upward at the sky and spread out on either side of him were a dozen soldiers, their rifles aimed and ready to fire. The officer's first attempt at a moustache did little to conceal his youth and he was clearly unused to armed confrontation.

He cleared his throat and, in as firm a voice as he could muster, called out, 'Gentlemen, I must order you to lay down your weapons and step out into the open.'

Swallowing their astonishment, Lamancha and Palliser-Yeates laid down their rifles and stood up straight. Faced with overwhelming firepower, their German opponents also dropped their guns and abandoned their cover.

The soldiers fanned out on both sides to surround the civilians. Some of them were clearly enjoying the opportunity to assert their military authority.

'Might I ask who you are?' Lamancha enquired.

'Lieutenant Ferrier, Seaforth Highlanders,' the young man answered. 'We were on manoeuvres up in the hills when we heard gunfire. You chaps seem to have started your own private little war.'

'War?' echoed Lamancha. 'No, no, it's all a misunderstanding. You see, my friend and I were trying to pot a few rabbits when a couple of shots went astray and hit those fellows' car. After that things got a bit heated.'

'Yes, dashed bad luck,' Palliser-Yeates confirmed. 'No harm intended, obviously.'

'And those gentlemen would be?' Lieutenant Ferrier asked, waving his pistol at Baron von Hilderling's party.

'Just a group of German tourists,' Lamancha answered quickly. 'Probably out seeing the sights.'

The baron's face was a mask of barely controlled fury. 'Yes, it is as he says, we are *holidaymakers*.' He ground out the word like a man forced to chew on lumps of chalk. 'It may be that we overreacted.'

'I'm afraid you can't have a gunfight and then simply walk away,' the lieutenant chided them censoriously. 'This isn't the Wild West, you know.'

'I know this doesn't excuse our folly,' said Lamancha, carefully drawing upon his deepest reserves of charm, 'but I'm Charles Lamancha, His Majesty's Secretary of State for the Dominions, and my friend here, Mr Palliser-Yeates, is one of our leading bankers. Perhaps we can smooth things over.'

'Perhaps you can, sir,' said Ferrier. 'That's not for me to say. Since the lot of you are more than I think the local constabulary can cope with, I'll have to ask you to accompany me back to Fort Donald and have a word with the general.'

'I have no time to visit your camp,' the baron snarled. 'I have urgent business to attend to.'

'I'm sure we all have important business, sir,' the lieutenant retorted curtly, 'but yours will just have to wait. I'm afraid I really must insist.' Turning to one of his men, he said, 'Corporal Rix, would you please go and fetch the lorry?'

Leaning towards Palliser-Yeates, Lamancha couldn't suppress a grin at the German's predicament. 'I can't say I relish the prospect of being corralled overnight in an army camp,' he said, 'but if it will take von Hilderling and his gang off the board, then it's a price worth paying.'

PART THREE

CASTLE MACNAB

17

THE DRY WELL

———

With the Kaiser safely locked away again, Kildennan provided Leithen and myself with food and water before devising a more ingenious prison for us. A rope was lowered to the bottom of the dry well and we were compelled at gunpoint to climb down it. When the rope was withdrawn the laird called down to us.

'Gentlemen, you'll bide safely there. Get yourselves some sleep and in the morning, after the deed is done, I'll leave you the means to climb out. You can then hike homeward and do whatever you will.'

His head and shoulders, a mere silhouette against the darkening sky, disappeared, and we were left alone in the shadowy depths.

'Sorry for putting you on the spot, Dick,' Leithen apologised.

He was only a vague shape in the gloom, but I could see he was leaning back against the wall of the well, as though glad at last to be free of the rigid demeanour of the courtroom.

'What, you mean as a surprise witness? It was a clever move on your part, even if I did feel pretty uncomfortable.'

'It was all I could think of to keep the trial going. And I still had some slight hope that if I could sow a few seeds of doubt in the mind of even one of those so-called jurymen, he might speak up for us.'

'If you'd been facing an impartial jury, Ned, you might

well have swung the verdict in our favour. But we knew from the start that their minds were made up, even if Wilhelm hadn't gone off on that last rant.'

'The poor old chap is quite bewildered,' said Leithen. 'He's still not over the shock of being forced to abdicate, even after all these years. He's quite convinced that God meant him to rule.'

'Divine right of kings and all that, eh? I hope he's not counting on God to get him out of this fix.'

We squatted down uncomfortably, relaxing as best we could under the cramped conditions. I wondered if the well had dried up before or after the massacre Kildennan had spoken of. Either way, this place certainly had a long-standing atmosphere of doom.

'Does Kildennan really plan to let us go?' I wondered. 'We're bound to report what he's done, after all.'

'Are we?' Leithen's question brought me up short. 'Once we're free, we still face the same dilemma as before. If we pass on what we know to the police and the government, what are they to do?'

'Do? They would arrest Kildennan, of course.'

'You think so? We already discussed the problem of finding an unwanted prisoner – the Kaiser – on their hands. Dealing with the diplomatic consequences of his death would be just as problematic.'

'Are you saying Kildennan is counting on the authorities hushing the whole thing up?'

'I don't think he cares one way or the other. Suppose he's arrested and prosecuted over this – he would throw himself before the court of public opinion. He's only done what many – perhaps most – people wanted done.

And he can justify it by the terms of the Versailles treaty, which called for the Kaiser to be tried.'

I realised that even in our present confined circumstances Leithen's ever-active mind had been exploring the many potential avenues that lay before us. Not for the first time I found myself admiring my friend's wide-ranging intellect.

'I agree there would be a fair amount of support for him,' I said, 'particularly among those who share his politics.'

'I think that support would go far beyond the membership of the National Banner movement. Remember how many of our newspapers carried the headline *Hang the Kaiser!* The government might well have to let the case drop in the interest of public order.'

'Are you saying putting him on trial would stir up a riot?'

'I'm saying he might get off scot free, and if not he would be a martyr for his cause, which might serve him even better.'

Following these sombre reflections, we were tired enough to eventually catch a few hours of broken sleep. Eventually I became too stiff and uncomfortable to doze. I picked myself up and stretched my aching back. As I did so, a thought crossed my mind.

'Ned?' I prompted.

'Yes?' he answered at once.

'Do you suppose they've set a guard?'

'I imagine they'll take turns on watch so they can all get some rest. The priority would be to guard the Kaiser's prison and keep an eye open for any more intruders. They reckon we're pretty well trapped down here.'

I guessed it must be close to three in the morning, so the chances were good that anyone on sentry duty would be less than fully alert. I stared up, straining my eyes to discern the narrow circle of the night sky beyond the well's rim.

'I think they've underestimated us,' I told my friend. 'They suppose that a lawyer will be a soft, city-bred sort, without the strength and skill to get out of this hole.'

'I can hardly blame them for thinking that,' said Leithen, pulling himself to his feet.

'Luckily they don't know about all the solo climbing you've done in the Alps. What do you reckon of this climb?'

'Maybe twenty-five feet. We've both climbed rocks a lot higher than that, but these walls don't have the natural crevices of a cliff face.'

I examined the stonework, moving my fingers up and down and from side to side. The stones were uneven and some had fallen out, creating a few handholds that might serve us.

'It feels to me as if there's enough to grip on so that we might just make it.'

Leithen made his own exploration of the well's sides and gave a grunt of agreement. 'We'll have to be pretty quiet about it. Let's hope that when we reach the top, whoever's on sentry duty has his back turned.'

'We need to overpower him without rousing the others,' I said, 'then free the Kaiser and get him out of here before anybody else stirs.'

Though I could not see him in the dark, I was sure my friend had a wry smile on his face. 'That doesn't sound so hard. Well, best not to hang about, eh?'

I explored with the toe of my boot until I found an exposed patch of earth. A couple sharp kicks created a cavity I could use to lever myself up while I dug my fingers into a space between the flat stones above my head. I could hear Leithen begin his ascent, keeping enough distance between us to prevent our accidentally jostling each other.

Toehold by toehold, crevice by crevice, I worked my way upward. Whenever my foot slipped or my fingers lost their grip, I had to bite back on my frustration and force myself to maintain complete silence. A straight vertical ascent is agonising on limbs and back and I wondered if by the time I reached the surface I would be in any condition to tackle any of our captors.

I could not look directly upward without losing purchase on the wall, so I had no way of judging my progress. I could hear Leithen scuffing and scraping as he struggled upward just a short distance below me. If either one of us got into difficulties there was nothing the other could do without hurling us both back down into the depths. Even with all my climbing experience, this was the most testing ascent I had ever attempted.

All at once we heard footsteps approaching and instinctively froze. We pressed ourselves flat against the stonework with our eyes shut tight so that they would not betray us by catching any gleam of light. The footfalls drew closer then paused. For a few breathless seconds there was silence, then we heard the invisible guard walking away. If he had taken a look down the well, he had not lingered long enough to penetrate the darkness.

I stifled a sigh of relief, fearful that even so small a

sound might give us away. Starting upward again, my muscles ached in protest, and it sometimes took me a full minute to find some hold I could use to progress another few inches. The gloomy thought occurred to me that Kildennan might not have overestimated the security of this makeshift prison.

We were so high now that a fall would probably do either one of us enough damage to make another attempt impossible. I kept telling myself it must be only a few more feet to the top, that soon the physical torment of this climb would be over. My fingers were cracked and bleeding from clawing at the stones and my cheek had been scraped raw against the rough surface. Every time I stretched out an arm or leg, my sinews felt ready to burst apart. I knew Leithen was silently suffering the same agonies and my determination not to let him down served to stiffen my resolve.

A minuscule change in the quality of the air alerted me to the fact that I was – finally – within reach of the top. Bending my neck back I saw only an arm's length away the edge of the outer ring of stonework. I wished I could pass this encouraging news on to Leithen, but even one word might give us away to whoever was patrolling above.

I flung an arm over the top, my fingers clutching the outer edge of the rock circle. I hauled myself up and over, striving to keep my breath contained. I had a brief moment of elation before I heard Leithen slip and scrabble, fighting for a hold. His frantic, rasping breaths told me he was in danger of plunging down all the way to the bottom.

I made a desperate lunge and seized him by the arm. With all the strength I had left, I dragged him up over the edge and we collapsed on the ground side by side, panting uncontrollably.

Out of the dark came a hushed, startled voice. 'Dinna ye move, gentlemen.'

I twisted about and saw young Roddy Strachan advancing steadily towards us, his rifle pointed at my head.

18

THE FALSE RUN

—

'Shoot us if you must,' Leithen growled hoarsely, 'but I'll not go back down in that hole.'

Though he held us at gunpoint, the boy had not raised the alarm, which gave me a sliver of hope.

'Roddy, listen, we have to get the Kaiser out of here.' I spoke as low as I could while still placing an urgent emphasis on my words. 'If your laird goes through with his plan there will be hell to pay.'

The pale moonlight illuminated the anguish in the young man's face. 'When my older brother Gavin was blinded in the war,' he recalled with a catch in his voice, 'the laird did everything for us, everything. I'll no' forget that, but this business is . . . wrang.'

He paused while Leithen and I kept silence, giving him space to complete his thought. He cast a troubled eye over the doom-laden oak that dominated the centre of the dead village, and almost shuddered.

'It's as Sir Edward says, war is too big and too terrible to put aw the blame o' it on just one man. Wha'ever that German might hae been in the past, now he's just a scared old man and nay harm tae onybody.'

'So you'll let us go then?' Leithen appealed quietly.

I hoped the lad wouldn't need more persuading than that. Though we were talking in hushed voices, every word spoken increased the danger of discovery.

The boy licked his lips and nodded. 'Aye. Sometimes

daein' the right thing is grievous hard, but I'll dae it.'

He turned his back and tossed his cap aside. 'Gi'e me a crack on the heid wi' ane o' yon stanes, hard enough for me tae mak oot as how I was knocked daft.'

We got to our feet and I picked up one of the many rocks littering the ground. 'Thanks, Roddy. It's a brave thing you're doing.'

He appeared deaf to my approval. 'Ye'll no tak my gun, tho'. I'll no hae ye shootin' any o' oor folk.'

'I promise,' I said, drawing back my arm. 'And thanks again.'

I took a swing and smacked him across the back of the head. He flopped down on his belly with his rifle trapped beneath him. I hoped he was only feigning unconsciousness and that I had not done him any serious injury.

As quietly as we could manage, Leithen and I hurried to the cottage where the Kaiser was imprisoned. Now that we were out in the open air we shook off the pains of our climb and felt our strength rapidly returning.

We carefully lifted the wooden bar from the door and laid it on the ground. Once inside I spotted the vague outline of the Kaiser's slight frame curled up on the straw beneath the window. I shook him gently awake and clamped a hand over his mouth to keep him from crying out. Even in the dark I noticed that his eyes were wide with fear, assuming that his executioners had come for him.

'Steady, sir. It's me, Hannay,' I told him. 'Leithen is with me. We're going to get you out of here, but you must keep quiet or you'll rouse Kildennan and his crew.'

He nodded to indicate that he understood and I removed my hand from his face. 'There will be confusion in the ranks of my enemies,' he muttered as he struggled to rise.

I helped him to his feet and led him outside to where Leithen crouched by the open doorway, keeping watch. Before we could make another move, an anxious voice shook the night air.

'Roddy! Roddy! Where are ye, boy?'

We saw the burly figure of the elder Strachan striding across the centre of the village with his back to us. Whether some fatherly instinct had alerted him to his son's situation or whether this was a prearranged change of watch, I could not tell. I was thankful that Roddy's slumped figure was not easily distinguished from the heaps of rubble dotted about the place.

Supporting the Kaiser between us, Leithen and I pulled him round to the rear of the cottage out of sight.

'Roddy, what's happened to ye?' Strachan exclaimed.

I realised that he had found his son at last and was probably attempting to rouse him.

'Once he wakes the rest of them, there's no way we can get Wilhelm clear without being spotted,' I whispered to my friend.

Leithen's nimble mind was racing, quickly calculating our options. 'You keep him hidden back here, Dick. I'll lead them away, and once they've cleared out you two make for the rendezvous at Castle Crachan.'

I was appalled at the thought of Leithen drawing Kildennan's huntsmen after him, but there was no time to consider alternatives. He had already slipped off into the shadows and started working his way around southward to the opposite side of the village.

I risked a peep round the edge of the cottage and saw Strachan bending over his son, trying to revive him. Roddy was doing his best for us by taking his time coming round. Finally he groaned, 'Father?' and tried to sit up, rubbing the back of his head where I had struck him.

The elder Strachan grabbed the boy's rifle and fired a shot in the air. This brought Kildennan, Mackinnon and Anderson dashing out from where they had been lying among the ruins wrapped in their sleeping blankets.

There was a heated exchange of words, then Kildennan scooped up a handful of stones and flung them down the well. The only sound was of them pattering on the empty bottom, confirming that we had escaped our prison.

I drew back out of view and put a finger to my lips to keep the Kaiser silent. He pressed his knuckles to his mouth and huddled against the wall.

'Damn them!' Kildennan cursed. 'I'd have sworn nothing but a monkey could climb out of that pit!'

'Oh, Roddy,' sighed Strachan, 'how could you let them sneak up on you?'

Roddy merely groaned in reply and I heard Mackinnon dash into the open cottage to confirm that the prisoner was gone. As he burst out again to report, Anderson raised a cry.

'Look, there's one of them running up that slope!'

From the distance I heard Leithen shout as though to someone up ahead of him, 'Keep going, Dick! Get the old fellow clear! I'll hold them off if I have to!'

Fully awake in the clear light of day, it might have

occurred to our captors that we could have split up, but in the heat of the moment they took off in furious pursuit. I risked a look and saw them charging off after Leithen, who had already passed out of sight.

Leithen, I knew, had won the mile at Eton and was a second string for the quarter at Oxford. Since then he had kept himself in shape with rigorous exercise and regular expeditions to the Swiss Alps. He had prodigious reserves of stamina and an uncanny instinct for finding his way through the most treacherous terrain. If anyone could elude these determined hunters, he was the man, but it would be a near-run thing.

I turned to the Kaiser. 'Right, we need to get out of here before they realise Leithen is acting as a decoy.'

He clutched at my arm as I started to move.

'There is a boat waiting for me at a place called . . .' his brow creased in concentration, 'Barrowstone?'

'Barrastane,' I corrected him. 'That's a fair hike from here. Look, I've arranged a rendezvous with some friends of mine at Castle Crachan, which is some ten miles due west. If they're waiting for us there, they can help us shake loose of Kildennan.'

Wilhelm nodded his acquiescence to my plan. How odd it was to be issuing orders to a man who, when we first met years ago, was commanding the most ruinous war the world had ever seen.

We headed westward through the trees and into the hills. I was glad to turn my back on that village, which had so nearly become the scene of a cruel execution. I had felt pity for Wilhelm back in 1916 and now it was even more obvious that he was merely a vain, foolish man unsuited to the great responsibilities he had been born to. How many men would have made a better job of it, were they subjected to the same Prussian upbringing with its culture of militaristic pride and rigid authoritarianism?

I did my best to use the constellations to keep us on course and was glad to hit the odd deer trail with its easier footing. Even so, it was slow going in the dark, with tree roots and rabbit holes waiting to trip us, and every owl hoot giving us a start, so alarmed were we at the prospect of our captors' catching up with us. Once I almost toppled over a badger as he snuffled along seeking out some worms for his supper. I envied him the fact that he had a nearby sett to hide in when the sun rose.

Our progress was further hindered by how much these past couple of days had taken out of my companion. He was no longer the jaunty figure I had spotted hiking through the hills. Now he lagged and stumbled, and there were times he seemed to have forgotten even where he was. I did not doubt that he had slept little during his captivity, so that now an inevitable fatigue threatened to overtake him.

As dawn lit the edges of the sky, a mass of black clouds rolled overhead to smother the rising sun. I had seated Wilhelm on a boulder to rest when the first raindrops began to fall.

'Come on, we need to get to higher ground,' I said, drawing him gently to his feet.

'Ach! Even your Scottish weather is against me,' he muttered.

In front of us lay a wooded ridge. We struggled uphill through a downpour that grew heavier by the minute. The noise of the rain beating down all around grew as loud as the roar of an incoming tide. Suddenly Wilhelm caught my arm and I thought at first it was to keep himself from slipping and falling. Then I saw he was pointing ahead with a feverish intensity in his eyes.

'Look, Hannay, look! There is a building ahead!'

I peered through the grey, sodden air and spied beyond a stand of pine trees a wall of stone that suggested a structure of some sort, perhaps an old bothy or a huntsman's lodge.

The prospect of gaining shelter put a spring in both our steps and we slogged over the muddy ground with our gaze fixed on our destination.

As we drew closer I heard the Kaiser groan. He might have crumpled to the ground if he had not been using my arm for support. What we had thought was a man-made structure was just a cliff face riven with strata so straight and regular they gave the appearance of human construction. With the crushing of hope, Wilhelm collapsed against me.

'An illusion,' he moaned. 'It was all a vile illusion.'

I wasn't certain if he was speaking of the deceptive cliff face or the whole mad enterprise of seeking to recover his throne.

'We need to keep going,' I urged, wrapping an arm around him. 'Come on!' He felt very small and frail in my grasp.

The awful thought occurred to me that the hardships he had suffered and the torrent beating down on us might yet do for him as surely as Kildennan's rope.

19

A MIGHTY FORTRESS

———

The water coursing over rock and earth rendered the footing treacherous and I stumbled more than once. The Kaiser staggered along, clinging to my arm and soon I realised I would be forced to carry him if we were to keep going. Following the stratified cliff face, I spotted a patch of deeper dark that gave me a sudden ray of hope.

Some words of encouragement kept the Kaiser on his feet for a few more yards, and then I saw I was not deceived. A short distance ahead a natural concavity in the rock looked deep enough to provide us with some cover.

I pushed my companion in ahead of me and we slumped down together on a layer of loose shale in a space not much larger than a broom cupboard. There was just enough of an overhang in the rock above us to form a roof of sorts. Beyond our outstretched feet the rainfall continued to thrash the ground so hard we could see the drops bouncing.

With a shiver the Kaiser drew up his knees to huddle himself into a miserable heap. I did my best to angle my body so that it shielded him from the incoming draughts of damp air.

Presently he stirred and raised his head. 'Oh, my friend, my friend,' he sighed, 'what have I come to?'

'Just rest,' I advised him. 'Close your eyes and we'll push on once the rain's passed.'

I hoped he would sleep and recoup some of his lost energy, but instead he let his tongue run on, as though he were making a speech, one he had prepared for those supporters he had imagined were waiting to greet him.

'I never wanted to abdicate. It was forced upon me. The allied powers would not make peace otherwise, so they said. So our self-seeking politicians and corrupt business men dragged me from the throne. And what is the result? A nation in ruins, without guidance, without the vision of a divinely ordained leader.'

I supposed that, given all he was going through, it was only natural that he should cast himself in the role of victim rather than the perpetrator of wrongs visited upon other people. He continued in this vein until I thought he was no longer sensible of my presence, but then he looked directly at me.

'Did you know, Hannay, that when my wife, my Dona, died a few years ago, I could not attend her funeral? No, she was buried in our homeland where I am forbidden to set foot. Can you even think what that was like?'

I recalled those occasions when I had been separated from my own dear Mary and had to contemplate the possibility that we might never see each other again. It was a feeling common to men in war.

'It was painful, I'm sure,' I responded with genuine sympathy.

He turned his face away from me and peered moodily out at the rain beating down beyond the confines of our tiny shelter. After a moment, he resumed his earlier resentful tone.

'Do you know who those swine are who have made me

into a hunted dog? Those plotters who have worked long and hard for my destruction?' When I remained silent, he supplied his own answer. 'I speak of course of the Freemasons and their allies the Catholic Church.'

It was disturbing to hear his sense of persecution drifting further and further from reality. I hardly knew what to say in the face of his ravings, but he needed no prompting from me to continue.

'For so long they have watched for their chance. Yes, they engineered my downfall for one purpose, to replace the Protestant house of Hohenzollern with a Catholic dynasty, with a puppet king who would dance to the will of the Pope.'

As far as I was aware, there were no plans to establish a Catholic dynasty in Germany, but I knew it was futile to try to reason with my companion. He was in the grip of what I have heard referred to as an *idée fixe*.

'That is why I must risk everything to return home,' he said, making a fist of his right hand, 'for the good of my people. *I will walk among you and ye shall be my people. Walk ye in all the ways I have commanded you for without me ye can do nothing.* Those are the very words of Scripture, Hannay, and I would that my people would listen.'

'But surely,' I said, hesitating even to utter the words, 'surely that passage refers not to any man but to . . . God?'

Wilhelm said nothing. His eyes had taken on a faraway look, as if I, along with our surroundings, had become a mere mist, dissolving before the clarity of his vision. It was his own imagined future he was gazing upon, a glory that belonged solely and privately to him.

Was this the passing delusion of an exhausted mind? Or behind the pain and broken dignity of a fallen monarch, were these the thoughts that lurked in the very depths of his soul? I had seen the rigours of war and the shock of battle affect men in different ways according to their temperament. Some rose to heights of heroism they had not known they were capable of. Others were driven into a sullen, savage dementia, making them easy prey to the most dreadful fantasies.

'You are a Scotsman and a good Protestant,' said Wilhelm, patting my arm. 'We are allies, you and I, allies against the ancient enemy.'

A more immediate enemy occupied my thoughts. The storm would delay Kildennan's pursuit, but the wet, muddy ground would make us easier to track. How I wished it would stop raining, and how I wished my companion would stop talking.

'When I return to Germany,' Wilhelm's voice dropped to a hoarse whisper, 'I shall see that those traitors pay for their crimes. All of those who rejected me – who stole my crown and drove me from my kingdom – all will be punished.'

The prospect of inflicting a cruel chastisement on his own people brought a faint smile to his lips and his eyes drooped. A welcome silence descended upon our little shelter, leaving me to stare out at the curtain of rain, knowing that somewhere out there Leithen was struggling through the storm. With any luck Lamancha and Palliser-Yeates were out there too, hurrying to our aid.

At last the downpour passed and a few wan shafts of sunlight poked feebly through the clouds. I roused

Wilhelm and helped him clamber out of our cramped little nook. Estimating our direction from the watery sun, we set out westward at a good speed. Having vented his hatred of his supposed enemies, Wilhelm appeared to draw strength from his determination to visit a terrible revenge upon them. I found a broken tree limb that he could use as a staff in place of his lost alpenstock and this too seemed to brighten his spirits.

It was past noon when I caught sight of Loch Dhuie, a smooth expanse of grey beneath the cloudy sky. The surrounding purple hillsides were dully reflected in its unbroken surface. I pointed it out to my companion, who seemed to have difficulty focusing on the distance. By now he was leaning on me as heavily as on his makeshift staff.

A rough-hewn crag loomed over the loch shore. From the distance it resembled the skull of a fallen giant, with the remains of Castle Crachan perched atop it like a crumbling stone crown.

Between us and the castle lay broken ground seamed with gullies and barred with stands of sessile oak and downy birch. The branches of the gaunt trees had been twisted and withered by winter gales until they looked like the black skeletons of dead witches.

I carefully guided the Kaiser through the many obstacles that lay in our path until we stood at the foot of the crag, gazing up the shattered remains of the ancient castle. With his right arm wrapped around my neck, we clambered up the steep, rocky slope until, with only a few yards to go, a welcome voice hailed us from above.

'Dick! Praise the Lord you made it!'

It was Leithen beaming down on us through a gap in what remained of the outer wall. I was not surprised that he had arrived ahead of us. Though his circuitous route had obliged him to make a longer journey, he was unhindered by an enfeebled companion, and so was able to travel at his own much faster pace.

Once I was at his side we each took an arm to haul the Kaiser up the last stretch. 'Welcome to Castle Crachan,' Leithen greeted him.

'Ah, my good lawyer!' Wilhelm responded with a lopsided grin. He stumbled past us into the centre of the ruins where he leaned gratefully against a wall mottled with lichen.

'Kildennan?' I enquired of my friend.

'I made a feint towards his place,' said Leithen, 'so he'd think I was trying to get to my car. Luckily I found a gully that kept me out of sight while I cut back west and north to meet you.'

'You've not spotted any sign of him since?'

'No, but in this sort of country a man might be right behind you hidden by a dip in the ground or a stand of trees. There's no telling how near or far he might be.'

'No sign of Lamancha then?'

Leithen shook his head. Leaning in close, he asked, 'How is the old man doing?'

I decided not to burden my friend with the fevered imaginings that had been swirling through the Kaiser's disordered mind.

'Sometimes I think he's going to expire from sheer despair,' I answered. 'At other time he seems possessed of an absolute mania that's driving him beyond the limits of his endurance.'

Wilhelm was stumbling unsteadily among the stubbled rocks of the castle interior. He gazed wonderingly about him as if the ancient structure were still completely intact, providing him with unassailable protection.

'*Ein feste Burg ist unser Gott!*' we heard him exclaim in his own tongue. 'You know the hymn, my friends? It was composed by Luther himself and for centuries our soldiers have sung it as they marched into battle – *a mighty fortress is our God.*'

He patted the mossy stump of a broken pillar and emitted a cracked laugh. 'This shall be our fortress, eh? Here even the ultimate enemy shall not prevail against us.'

I walked over and tried to guide him to a sheltered spot. 'Look, I really think you should sit down and calm yourself.'

He clutched the front of my coat with claw-like fingers and fixed his bulging eyes upon me. 'You know who they are, of course – of course you do. The Elders of Zion!' He spat the words. 'They are behind all the evils of the world.'

I was shocked by the venom in his voice. I had heard this sort of rot before but always assumed it would die away in time like the belief in goblins and witchcraft.

'They pitched our two nations into war so that we might destroy each other,' he hissed with bitter intensity. 'And upon the ruins of our cities they will raise up their accursed temples.'

His voice trailed off abruptly and he swayed on his feet. With one accord Leithen and I darted forward to catch him as he began to swoon. We supported him to a corner of one of the old rooms and set him down where he could not be seen from below.

'Take it easy, sir,' I soothed him. 'Help is on the way, so we'll keep an eye out.'

Wilhelm made no answer. Elbows on his knees, he slumped forward, his glazed eyes directed at the cracked flagstones between his feet. Leaving him to his twisted delusions, Leithen and I took up position at the foot of a hollow tower where we had a clear view of the landscape below.

Once we were out of earshot, Leithen voiced his dismay. 'Is he sick in the head,' he wondered, 'or does he really believe that hateful rubbish?'

'You and I both know that under the stress of battle men will sometimes spew out the most outrageous nonsense,' I said. 'Unfortunately for him, this isn't exactly a rest cure.'

Leithen cast a pitying glance back at the slumped figure of the old Kaiser. 'Well, if he's losing his mind, that's all the more reason to protect him against Kildennan's vengeful mockery of justice.'

I began to assess our chances of protecting our charge, given that we had cover and the high ground. 'This isn't much of a mighty fortress, but we may be forced to make a stand here.'

'We wouldn't be the first,' Leithen informed me, ever the historian. 'In the fourteenth century Sir Darius Rintoul, a supporter of Robert the Bruce, died defending this castle against the enemies of his chosen king. After that it was left to fall into ruins.'

'Well, I hope we have better luck than Sir Darius,' I said. 'Maybe we should rename the place Castle Macnab.

That name seems to bring good fortune with it.'

'I wish the rest of the Macnabs were here,' Leithen sighed. 'Do you think we should stay holed up here or press on?'

'I don't think Wilhelm's up to another trek,' I said. 'If we could rustle up a boat we could transport him over the loch.'

Leithen silenced me with a warning hand. 'Hang on – somebody's coming.'

We ducked out of sight and I peered towards the south where a pair of shadowy figures were picking their way through the trees. 'What do you think? Is it Lamancha or Kildennan?'

20

SEPARATE ROADS

The engine of the Hispana coughed twice as it coasted to a halt on the eastbound road some miles to the south of Castle Crachan. Tied to its rear was a rusty bicycle. Janet had found it in the back storeroom of Rushforth Lodge and insisted on bringing along.

Archie alighted from the car and gazed northward over the rain-soaked landscape that stretched all the way to Loch Dhuie. When Janet and Ilsemann joined him, he pointed out the expanse of heather-clad hillocks, thick woodland and sodden ground that lay before them.

'There's no way we can drive through that without getting bogged down,' he told them. 'We've lost a lot of time already, what with that storm and the engine packing up a couple of times.'

The car had taken some damage during the flight from Kinclavers and there had been little time for repairs.

'It looks like a rough trek, Archie,' Janet observed. 'What's the plan?'

Her husband set his jaw decisively. 'If the captain and I hop to it, we should reach the castle in a couple of hours.'

'Then we must set off without delay,' Ilsemann urged. 'Every passing second is vital.'

'I still say somebody should scout out Castle Kildennan,' said Janet. 'We might pick up the trail from there.'

'What, stick our heads in the lion's mouth?' said Archie. 'No fear. Besides, Charles was quite clear that we should make for the rendezvous point at Castle Crachan.'

'I suppose you're right,' Janet conceded, but there was a glint of mutiny in her eyes.

Leaning back against the passenger door of the car, she looked on quietly as the two men grabbed their packs, which were filled with water bottles, food and a first aid kit.

'Now you stand guard over the old bus,' Archie instructed her. 'We'll be back as quickly as we can and with any luck we'll have the rest of the gang with us.'

'Take a kiss for luck first,' Janet insisted, pulling him close.

Ilsemann looked discreetly away as husband and wife made their goodbyes, then he and Archie struck out across the wild countryside.

Janet waited until they were out of sight, then quickly unstrapped the bicycle from the back of the Hispana. In a matter of seconds she was pedalling furiously in the direction of Castle Kildennan.

'Women are extraordinary creatures, don't you think?' mused Archie as he and Ilsemann squelched through a boggy mass of dock weed.

'They are the kinder face of humanity,' Ilsemann agreed. 'When I lay bound in that hotel room, expecting my imminent death, I thought frequently of my dear Elizabeth back at Amerongen. I wished for nothing more than to hold her hand one last time.'

'Like most men I'm basically a bit of a clod,' Archie chuckled self-deprecatingly, 'but there are three things capable of ennobling a chap like me: God, a good school, and a woman's love. I expect God's done his best and can't be blamed for the result, and I never really took to school. But Janet's kindled something new in me. Thanks to her I feel I could chip in on the search for the Holy Grail and hold my own along with Galahad and the rest of the knightly crew.'

'It is perhaps the spirit of King Arthur that makes you Tommies such magnificent soldiers,' said Ilsemann.

'Really?' Archie was pleased at the compliment. 'I thought your Kaiser said we were *contemptible*.'

'That is a misunderstanding.' Ilsemann waved the insulting word aside. 'He referred only to the size of your army not its quality. No, no, we admired your troops and – let me say in all truthfulness – we *liked* them.'

'Even when you were shelling us?' Archie asked dubiously.

'Even then,' said Ilsemann. 'Your soldiers were always so well turned out compared to other armies, and always properly shaved. In fact, we looked forward to capturing your trenches because we knew we would find plenty of soap and shaving equipment. We appreciated those, for towards the end we had no more ourselves.'

'I'm glad we could oblige you,' Archie joked. He took a bar of chocolate from his pocket, broke off a piece and handed it to his companion. 'You chaps are no slouches in a scrap either, but I suppose sheer British pluck prevailed in the end.'

Ilsemann crunched up his chocolate and swallowed. 'It was not your *pluck* that defeated us, it was your Lord Northcliffe.'

'Northcliffe? The chap with all the newspapers?'

'Just so. Always we were subjected to his most constant and duplicitous propaganda. Your Lord Northcliffe with his newspapers pounded us day after day like the bombardment of artillery. He raised anger against us and sapped the morale of our own people. If we had such a man, such a genius for twisting the truth to his own ends and spreading it abroad, with such a man on our side, we would have won the war.'

Archie munched quietly on his own piece of chocolate as he listened to this unexpected assessment of the allied victory.

'Well, we're all done with the war now, eh?' he said at last. 'What I don't understand, Siggy, is why you've chosen to shut yourself up in exile with your former Kaiser. Surely for a chap like you there must be lots of opportunities for promotion and advancement back in Germany.'

The slightest flicker of uncertainty passed across Ilsemann's face. After a moment's pause he said, 'The emperor is just a man like you or me, but there is nothing ordinary about the burden the world has laid upon his shoulders. It is my duty to remain by his side and see that he never loses sight of that better part of his nature which is sometimes clouded over by the many misfortunes he has suffered.'

'Yes, you chaps are very big on duty,' Archie observed.

'Without duty,' Ilsemann asserted stiffly, 'without loyalty, we are no better than the savages.'

Janet leapt from the bicycle and let it clatter to the ground in the driveway of Castle Kildennan. She bounded up the front steps and gave the bell-pull a violent tug. As soon as the door opened, she brushed past the timid maid and marched into the hallway.

'Hello!' she called. 'Is anybody home or are you all out hunting?'

The maid followed, her hands pressed nervously to her cheeks. 'Madam, please . . .'

'It's all right, Margaret,' came a voice, 'you can get back to work.'

A tall, auburn-haired young woman had emerged from the library with a huge wolfhound padding along at her heels. She carried herself with an air of invincible authority. As the maid scurried off, Janet met the mistress of the house. 'Miss Kildennan, Christina Kildennan?'

'We've met, I believe. Janet Raden, isn't it?'

'I recently married,' said Janet. 'My husband is Sir Archibald Roylance.'

'I suppose I must congratulate you, Lady Roylance,' said Christina without warmth. 'But shouldn't you be with your husband, not raising a halloo here in my house?'

Janet met her gaze squarely. 'You know very well why I'm here.'

Swinging on her heel, Christina led the way into the library and shut the door behind them. She closed a leather-bound book that lay open on the desk and placed it back on its shelf. She said frostily, 'I'm afraid you have the advantage of me. Is the parish organising a bazaar? Or do you wish me to subscribe to one of your charities?'

'I didn't come here to make small talk,' Janet retorted. She was aware of the massive dog circling her but kept her attention directed firmly on the other woman. 'My friends Richard Hannay and Edward Leithen came here to rescue the old Kaiser from your father's murderous intent. You know that as well as I, and I want to know what has become of them.'

Christina turned her back to pour herself a brandy from a decanter. She took a sip before facing her unwanted guest once more.

'You think yourself very well informed, it seems, and well placed to pass judgement on my father.'

A fierce, elemental cold seemed to gather about the young Lady Kildennan. It was almost as though she were standing in the middle of a bare, storm-blasted moor and not in the comfortable confines of wood-panelled library. Janet felt a palpable chill as she took a step closer. The great hound loped to his mistress's side and sank down on his haunches like a guard on watch.

Janet chose her words with care. 'I understand your father's grief and your loyalty to him, but don't you see it's gone beyond that now?'

'No one asked you or any of your friends to interfere,' Christina stated flatly. 'If you have any sense you will go home to Strathlarrig. I'm sure your family would be pleased to see you.'

'Do you expect us to simply stand by and let this crime unfold?' Janet challenged her. 'That may be fine for you, but we expect better of ourselves.'

Christina tossed back the last of her drink and slammed the glass down on the table. 'Do you think I choose to be an observer in all this? Do you believe it suits my nature to bide at home waiting for news?'

'Then don't stay here,' said Janet. 'There is still time to do something – or is the Kaiser already dead?'

Christina stiffened, as though preparing for a plunge into icy water. 'Your friends broke loose last night. They escaped, taking the old man with them. My father sent young Roddy back here to tell me, part of his punishment for his carelessness.'

'My husband is out there looking for them,' said Janet. 'If your father catches up to them, Hannay and Leithen won't back down and Archie will stick with them to the end.'

The mistress of the house was unyielding. 'Then he's a fool, and so are they to stand in my father's way when they could easily step aside. And why will they not? The only loss to the world will be one evil old man.'

'Is that what you want, another death to numb your pain?' Janet's blue eyes flashed with a determined ferocity. 'Do you really suppose that all the thousands and thousands of ghosts out there want more company? Or do they value every living breath as something more precious than you and I can even imagine, no matter who's breathing it?'

Christina paced the floor and her fingers drifted up unconsciously to touch the black ribbon that bound her hair. 'Even if anything could be done, how are we to find them? They could be anywhere by now.'

The hound sprang up and stood quivering, his sharp eyes darting back and forth between the two women.

'I know where they're headed,' said Janet. 'If we can get there in time . . . '

'Those are armed men out there,' Christina pointed

out. 'You'll not deflect them from their purpose.'

Janet closed the distance between them but stopped short of reaching out to the other woman. Her face flushed with a righteous passion. 'If you could save the life of someone you loved, would you not be willing to destroy everything that stood in your way?'

Christina turned abruptly aside to stare out of the window at the rain-sodden garden. Her hazel eyes filled with a haunted mist, as though she were gazing upon a battlefield of the dead and remembering a place she had never been. For the first time her voice wavered. 'I was never granted the opportunity.'

Janet felt an answering pang in her heart. 'Yes, I know, and I'm sorry. But my Archie is the most good-hearted man on the face of the earth. I'm going out there and I'll stand in the way of any danger – fire, bullets or lightning – in order to bring him safely home.'

Turning from the window, Christina started at what she saw. The great hound Fearghal had padded over to the other woman and was rubbing his muzzle gently against her leg. Janet reached down to scratch his shaggy head and the dog uttered a friendly rumble.

Christina placed a hand on her throat and the two women locked eyes. An understanding as old as the world passed between them as a gust of wind rattled the windows and a lone kestrel flew screeching overhead.

After a moment's hesitation, Christina strode across the room and out into the hall. 'Roddy!' she yelled. 'Roddy! Run to the stables and saddle a pair of horses. Lady Roylance and I are going for a ride!'

21

THE ASSAULT ON CASTLE MACNAB

I peered intently into the gloom, straining to perceive whether the newcomers were friend or foe. Just as they emerged from the shadow of the trees a familiar voice rang out.

'Hello! Is anybody home?'

To my utter astonishment, I recognised Archie Roylance as he began climbing the steep slope below the castle. With him was another young man I had never seen before, who tackled the ascent with vigorous haste. Leithen and I reached down to give them a helping hand over the last few feet.

'Archie, what on earth are you doing here?' I greeted my friend.

Archie had been one of my subalterns in the Lennox Highlanders before leaving to join the Flying Corps and our paths had crossed many times since.

'It's rather a lengthy story,' Archie replied, 'but first let me introduce Captain Sigurd von Ilsemann, the Kaiser's adjutant. Siggy, this is Dick Hannay and Ned Leithen. You couldn't wish for better company in a tight spot.'

'We're definitely in a tight spot,' Leithen confirmed.

Ilsemann returned our greeting with a perfunctory nod. 'The emperor, he is safe?'

'He's over there.' I turned to see the Kaiser heave himself from the ground and stagger towards us.

'Sigurd! Sigurd!' he gasped at the sight of a welcome, familiar face.

'Try to get him to rest,' I urged Ilsemann. 'We may not be through the worst of this yet.'

The young officer took Wilhelm by the arm and led him back to where he could be seated. While he unpacked some welcome food and drink for his master, they conversed together in their own language, their voices too low for me to pick up.

Archie filled me in on his encounter with Lamancha and Palliser-Yeates, and his and Janet's subsequent adventures right up to the point where he and the young German had set out on foot to find us.

'What do you make of this Ilsemann?' Leithen asked Archie when he had finished his tale.

'Siggy?' Archie shrugged off-handedly. 'He has some queer ideas about the war, but I can't help liking the chap.'

'That's good enough for me, Archie,' I said. 'And Lord knows we need all the help we can get.'

Archie brought out some bannocks and cheese from his pack. While we gratefully tucked in, he said, 'Janet's back there keeping an eye on the car and with any luck Charles and John have shaken off that dratted baron and are on their way here. So what's your plan, chaps?'

'I really don't think we can hang about here,' said Leithen. 'It's only a matter of time before Kildennan picks up our trail.'

'Look, it will take an hour or two to hike back to my car,' Archie offered, 'but once there we can drive to wherever we choose.'

'Now that Captain von Ilsemann is here,' I said, 'it may be possible to keep the Kaiser on the move.'

'I agree,' said Leithen. 'We've got to chance it. Between the four of us, we can carry the old man if we have to.'

'Right, chaps,' said Archie cheerfully, 'let's pack up and move out.'

He had no sooner spoken than the bark of a rifle cracked the air and a bullet smacked a chip out of the stonework only a couple of feet above my head. We all dived for cover at once. Two more warning shots followed, then came an ominous silence.

'It looks like we're staying put,' I surmised grimly.

Archie grimaced. 'I wish I'd brought my old pistol along on this trip.'

'We'd still be outgunned,' said Leithen. 'Besides, we don't want to get into a shooting war.'

'They're shooting already,' I pointed out.

'Just to keep us pinned down, I think,' said Leithen. 'They know we're unarmed and I think they'll still baulk at gunning down their own countrymen.'

'Suppose we make a break for it?' Archie suggested.

'We'd never make it unless we left the Kaiser behind,' I said. 'And Captain von Ilsemann isn't going to abandon him.'

The young German crawled over to us on his belly. 'What do we face now?' he asked.

'Four or five men, including Kildennan himself, all of them armed with rifles,' I told him.

Leithen's brow creased in thought. 'Look, Archie, you and the captain keep down out of sight,' he advised. 'They probably don't know you're here.'

I grasped what he was driving at. 'Yes, let them think there's only the two of us,' I said. 'If they don't know we have a strategic reserve, that could be our ace in the hole.'

'I've never been much use at cards,' Archie grinned, 'but I think I can hold my own in a scrap.'

'You can also count on me,' Ilsemann assured us before scrambling back to his master.

I was taking a swallow from the water bottle Archie had given me when I heard a booming command.

'Hannay! Leithen! Show yourselves!'

It was the deep, scornful voice of Kildennan. I peered over the edge of the castle wall to see him looking up at me from the top of a bare hillock about fifty yards off. He stood in the commanding pose of a general with a rifle cradled in his arms.

'You've led us a merry dance, Sir Edward,' he called, 'but I'll have done with this business by whatever means are required. Send the German out to me now and I'll leave you to depart in peace.'

Signalling Leithen to keep out of sight, I stood up so that our foe could see me. I trusted that the laird would not sink to the infamy of shooting me while we spoke.

'Kildennan, you've already pushed this as far as it will go. You've mistreated and terrorised an old man and threatened violence against your own countrymen. Let it rest. Don't carry this affair so far that matters can never be mended.'

'I've let your friend Leithen have his say,' Kildennan retorted, 'so I'll not stand here and let you preach at me. If you can't bring yourself to throw the German out here on the ground, then you can save some face by simply withdrawing. I offer a truce for the two of you to depart by whichever route you choose. I give you my word you will come to no harm and I will make no move to stop you.'

His arrogance added fire to my defiance. 'Are you saying we should simply abandon this man to your non-existent mercy? Are those the sort of cowards you take us for?'

'Whether you go or stay,' said Kildennan, 'it makes no difference. He will not leave this place alive. A wise man would cut his losses and make the best of it.'

If he was prepared to stand there and bluster, I was ready to spin out our dialogue. Certain that Lamancha and Palliser-Yeates must be be rushing to our aid, I knew it was in our interests to delay for as long as possible.

I answered him, hoping his men were listening. 'A wise man wouldn't hazard his daughter's future and the lives of his followers to fulfil his obsessive desire for revenge.'

Suddenly I heard Leithen address me with alarm in his voice. 'Dick, why is he wasting so much time on talk? Where are the rest of them?'

My heart lurched. Cursing my stupidity, I spun round to face the interior of the castle.

While Kildennan kept us distracted the three 'jurymen' had crept through the undergrowth and clambered stealthily up the loch side of the castle crag. Now they came vaulting over the fallen walls and charged us with a wordless battle cry like clansmen of old.

Somewhere in the course of their manhunt they had armed themselves with crude cudgels fashioned from broken tree limbs. Leading the way, Mackinnon took a swing at me but I managed to dodge below his club and drive my shoulder in his midriff. He staggered back, winded, but when I tried to follow up my advantage he landed a crack on my knee that almost felled me. Ignoring the pain, I dived for his legs and brought him down in a rugby tackle.

While we grappled on the ground, I saw Leithen take a painful whack on the head from the man Anderson's cudgel before Archie grabbed the lanky attacker from behind and wrestled him down. Peter Strachan – Roddy's grizzled father – was holding back to look for the Kaiser. He was more than surprised when Ilsemann came at him in a formal boxing stance and landed a hard blow on his chin.

Reeling from the hit he had taken, Leithen did his best to help Archie subdue and disarm Anderson. That cadaverous man landed a couple of good punches and scrambled out of their grasp. As soon as he got upright, Archie closed with him again, catching him in a headlock.

Dropping his cudgel, Mackinnon fought his way free of me and sprang to his feet. As I started to rise he treated me to a vicious kick in the ribs that knocked the wind out of me. Before he could follow up, Leithen caught him from behind with a punch to the kidneys that brought a malicious oath to his lips.

Strachan had abandoned his fight with Ilsemann and pulled Archie off Anderson. He bundled his two companions ahead of him, jumping the broken wall to rejoin their chief.

'There's too many!' he cried to his friends. 'Get out of here!'

As I clutched my aching ribs, I saw Kildennan clambering up the slope below with the rifle in his hands.

Strachan pelted down towards him at the head of the routed party. He grabbed the laird's rifle and pushed him back down to the foot of the crag.

'Not now, sir!' he gasped. 'It's not time for that yet.'

With a growl of frustration Kildennan let himself be dragged away and the whole gang disappeared into the trees to lick their wounds.

We had taken enough knocks ourselves to make it feel like something of Pyrrhic victory. I checked that there were no broken bones and saw that the Kaiser, shocked by the sudden assault, had retreated deep into his corner and curled up into a tight ball.

While Ilsemann tended to his master, the rest of us discussed our situation.

'That man Strachan may be misguided,' said Leithen, 'but I think he's doing his best to keep things from getting completely out of hand. They left their guns down below so there would be no shooting.'

'Perhaps they were afraid we'd wrestle the guns away from them as we did with these,' said Archie, proudly displaying a captured cudgel.

'Kildennan's not going to settle for fists and clubs next time he comes at us,' I said.

'Maybe we can set up some snares or rig up a slingshot,' said Leithen. He gave weary smile. 'Who'd have thought this old place would be the scene of another battle, or that we'd be holding our ground for the sake of a man who was once our greatest enemy?'

'I think that's where the heart of a soldier really rests,' I said. 'In one small patch of ground or with one person.' My mind went back to still-vivid memories of the last year of the Great War. 'From the moment I first met Mary in the garden at Fosse Manor, I knew what I was fighting for. Not for cause or country but for that house, that woman, and the future we would share together.'

'You found your promised land then, eh?' said Leithen. 'That holy ground the Greeks called a *temenos*.' I guessed from his expression that he had some special place of his own in mind. 'I rather think that's true of all of us: we all have some sacred spot from which we draw strength, whether a memory of the past or a vision of the future.'

'It seems to me that we can make even the scraggiest bit of earth a sacred place by our willingness to make a stand there,' said Archie, 'even this old ruin.'

'That's very well put, Archie.' I couldn't help but smile. 'I think that wife of yours is turning you into a bit of a philosopher.'

Archie groaned. 'Oh, please don't say that. All my other pals would give me the most brutal ragging if they heard that sort of talk.'

At that moment a fusillade of rifle fire sent bullets smacking into the stonework all around us. We were now truly at war.

22

THE WATCHERS

———

Janet and Christina rode out from Castle Kildennan, driving their horses as hard and fast as the steep and boggy terrain would allow. The young Lady Kildennan was mounted on her favourite, a powerful, impatient black stallion named Rinaldo. Janet had been given Britomart, a nimble chestnut mare who was far more amenable. She was an accomplished horsewoman, but she could tell that Christina exceeded her in skill, if not in her determination to reach their goal.

They were within sight of Castle Crachan's jagged walls when a volley of gunfire split the air. Both women reined in their mounts. Christina turned in the saddle and spoke firmly.

'Stay back here, Janet. There isn't any way you can reach your people without drawing fire and your presence might just make things worse. Let me go to my father alone and see what I can do.'

Much as she would have liked to dispute the point, Janet knew the other woman was right. Gritting her teeth, she said, 'Go then!', the words bursting out as though they had been ripped from her by force.

Christina was gone in an instant. Battling a sense of frustration, Janet swept her gaze over the surrounding terrain. Her eye was caught by an unexpected flicker of light on a wooded hilltop to her left.

She knew at once that someone was up there. The sun

had caught the lenses of the field glasses through which that person was observing the whole scene around Castle Crachan. Instinct more than reason spurred her on and she set off at a gallop towards that vantage point.

When she arrived on the height she saw two men. A pair of Highland ponies were tethered close by and a long-barrelled hunting rifle had been left leaning against a tree. As she slid down from the saddle the men swung round to face her and she recognised one of them at once, for the newspapers carried his photograph almost every day.

'Prince Edward,' she greeted him without deference.

Surprise at the approach of the young woman melted into a winning smile on the prince's handsome features as he laid his field glasses aside. His companion was a squarely built man with a large head of dark hair and an expansive brow. He studied Janet with the intelligent air of one who was scrutinising this change in the situation and reviewing its possibilities.

Janet narrowed her eyes at him. 'You must be Mr Warren Creevey. Lord Lamancha told me he'd met you both.' She turned back to the prince. 'He advised you to leave.'

There was an amused twinkle in Edward's eye. 'Oh, I'm never the first to leave the party. Besides, Mr Creevey and I had already arranged to go for a ride. When we heard the shots, we simply had to see what was going on.'

'Yes, I'm sure you were curious,' Janet responded curtly. Her mind was racing as she took in this new twist.

'I don't believe I've had the pleasure of making your acquaintance,' said the prince.

Janet lifted her chin. 'I'm Janet Roylance. My husband in Sir Archibald Roylance.'

'The local MP,' Creevey supplied.

'I've always found politics a bore myself,' Edward spoke with mock sympathy, 'but I suppose you get used to it.'

More scattered shots rang out below. Janet fixed an accusing glare on the prince. 'You! You are responsible for what's going on down there.'

Edward raised an ironic eyebrow. 'And what is that exactly?'

'You know that perfectly well.' Janet's voice had a sharp edge to it now. 'The former Kaiser of Germany is in that ruin, surrounded by men who mean to kill him. He would never have dared to come here without some guarantee from you. You are to blame for all of this.'

'This?' echoed the prince, casting a sardonic gaze over the scene below. 'This, no. I came up here for a chinwag with some old friends and a bit of a family reunion. We were going to chat about some future opportunities we might all benefit from. It's turned out to be rather a disappointment, hasn't it?'

He aimed a sidelong smirk at Warren Creevey, who did not appear to share the prince's flippancy. 'There have been some unfortunate developments,' the financier commented drily.

'My husband is down there along with some other brave men,' Janet told them. 'They have placed themselves between your German cousin and Lord Kildennan who might murder them in pursuit of his own warped justice. Are you going to just stand here and let it happen?'

'I never foresaw any of this,' Edward assured her, 'and I couldn't possibly get involved now. Lord knows I'm in enough trouble as it is. My father will be furious if he finds out.'

'You must go down there,' Janet informed him sternly. 'Kildennan will have to desist if you tell him to.'

'I'm sorry, but it is simply unacceptable for the prince to compromise himself any further,' Creevey stated dispassionately.

'Quite right,' Edward agreed, turning towards the ponies. 'In fact we should make ourselves scarce before things get any uglier.'

Janet reached the rifle in two swift strides and snatched it up. She levelled the weapon at the prince with shocking composure. 'Damn you, man, you will do what's honourable or I'll shoot you where you stand.'

With a menacing snap of the gun's steel bolt, she rammed a bullet into the chamber.

Edward met her gaze and saw two eyes that were as hard and unyielding as sword points. He swallowed and a cold sweat broke out upon his brow.

'I am your future king,' he reminded her.

'Only for a few seconds more if you don't do as I say.'

The blood of her warrior ancestors poured hot through Janet's veins now, so that she blazed with an almost unearthly power. Neither of the men who beheld her in awestruck horror doubted that she would lay waste to whole kingdoms in defence of those she loved.

Prince Edward ran the back of his hand across his dry lips and his voice died in his throat. There was a long, tense silence which Creevey finally broke.

'Perhaps it's not too late to make an adjustment to the situation.'

23

ARMS AND THE MAN

Gradually the gunfire subsided. There followed an eerie quiet broken only by the dank wind whispering through the surrounding foliage.

Archie made a game attempt at good cheer. 'Well, that's not the worst bombardment I've been through.'

'I think that was our last warning,' said Leithen. 'We've come to the edge at last.'

As if to fulfil his prediction, Kildennan's voice boomed out once more.

'I'm done with talking and fisticuffs. I give you five minutes to leave the field, then I'm coming for the old criminal myself and I'll shoot dead any man that stands in my way.'

'He means it,' I said. 'He's going to shoot to kill even if his men don't back him.'

'I hope to God they don't,' said Leithen grimly. 'Then at least we might have a chance of overpowering him.'

'I'm going to sneak down there,' I decided. 'If I can get my hands on just one of their guns, I might be able to swing things our way.'

Leithen laid a cautionary hand on my arm. 'That would almost certainly guarantee a shooting war, Dick. Perhaps we should stand our ground against him, unarmed as we are, and trust in the rightness of our cause.'

'You may be right, Ned,' I conceded, 'Kildennan might baulk at the last at the prospect of wholesale murder. But frankly I'm afraid that whatever beast is gnawing at his soul is determined to have its way.'

'I'll come with you, Dick,' Archie offered.

'No, Archie, you need to stay here. If I don't make it back, there will still be enough of you to mount a defence.'

I slid through a gap in the castle wall out of sight of the enemy and clambered down using boulders and bushes for cover. As I descended, I suddenly heard approaching hoofbeats and caught a glimpse of Christina Kildennan approaching astride a big black stallion. Reining in, she vaulted from the saddle and walked to where her father and his men were gathered.

When I reached level ground, I wriggled through the undergrowth towards them. My one hope was that they would not expect us to take the offensive and that I'd have surprise on my side.

Wet and muddy, I finally crawled into sight of Kildennan's party on the other side of a dense hawthorn bush. Mackinnon, with his back turned, was only a few feet away from me with a rifle in his hands. I decided at once that he would be my target.

Further off, Christina was making a desperate appeal to her father. Her voice was pitched so low, I could not make out her words, but it was clear from her anguished expression that they were heartfelt. I was just as clear that they were falling on deaf ears.

As I watched, Kildennan gave way to his pent-up fury. 'I'll hear no more of this wheedling talk!' he roared, and slapped her across the face with the flat of his hand. The young woman reeled back. Stunned more by the emotional betrayal than the force of the blow, she lost her footing in the wet grass and fell to the ground.

Her father made a move towards her, then checked himself. Strachan and Anderson helped their mistress up, but kept a grip on her arms to hold her back from any further confrontation.

Seizing on this moment of distraction, I jumped from cover and planted a mighty punch on Mackinnon's temple. As he went down like a felled ox, I grabbed the rifle out of his hands. Before I could make another move, however, Kildennan rounded on me with startling speed. He slammed his rifle butt into my chest and knocked me flat on my back. The captured weapon slipped out of my numbed fingers and he kicked it away out of reach.

The laird loomed over me, gun in hand, and eyed me like a hunter sizing up his prey. 'Hannay, will you never be done with standing in my way?'

With the wind knocked out of me, I could not even muster a word of defiance. I glanced towards Christina, who pressed a hand to her stinging cheek, her expression unreadable. Now that he had gone so far as to break the bonds of family, I feared that nothing we could do would restrain Kildennan from his intent.

A thin drizzle began to fall, filling the air with a damp, grey mist. As visibility shrank about us, I felt as though we had become unstuck in time and were caught in an endless cycle of conflict that had waged back and forth across this bleak landscape for untold centuries.

Then, as if conjured out of the past, a trio of ghostly figures materialised out of the mist, leading a pair of ponies and a chestnut mare. I was amazed to recognise Janet Roylance and, strolling a few paces ahead of her, the Prince of Wales.

The prince's relaxed, pleasant voice seemed to come from another reality.

'Right, everyone, let's try to cool off, shall we?'

I rose slowly to my feet, anxious not to make any sudden provocative move. I saw Kildennan gape at the prince, as though he were an apparition like Banquo's ghost. 'Your Highness, I had not expected . . .'

'Yes, I do turn up in the oddest places, don't I?' From Edward's manner you would have thought they had just run into each other at a cocktail party. 'Haven't seen you in an age, Kildennan. You really must drop by the palace for drinks. I've just picked up a case of really first class port.'

Whatever nerves he might be feeling, the prince was making an admirable show of calm authority. He lit a cigarette and blew a stream of smoke into the misty air.

Warren Creevey was watching this performance with the air of a detatched observer. Janet by contrast was all tension, and it was clear to me that if the occasion called for it she was ready to use the rifle she carried at her side.

'Now I don't doubt there has been a lot of unpleasantness,' Prince Edward continued, 'but it's nothing that can't be smoothed over. Don't you agree, Kildennan?'

The laird's face was a mask of tortured confusion. For a moment it looked as though he might turn his rifle on the prince, but he lowered it instead. Here was a line he could not cross without dishonour. His shoulders slumped and his shaggy eyebrows drooped. 'It's as you say, Your Highness,' he muttered.

'It would be best for everyone if none of this became public,' said Creevey. 'You can rest assured, Lord Kildennan, that there will be no repercussions for you or your family if you let this matter drop.'

'Absolutely. If there's one thing I've plenty of experience with, it's covering up a scandal.' Edward chuckled at his own joke.

Kildennan lifted his hollow gaze to the prince's face. 'When you're king,' he pleaded hoarsely, 'never take us into another war.'

Edward dropped his cigarette onto the damp grass at his feet and his smile faded. 'I'll do my best,' he said with a slow, solemn nod. 'I can assure you of that.'

The laird turned to his daughter and all but crumpled with grief at the sight of her cheek, bright red where he had struck her. 'Oh, Kirsty, will you ever forgive me?'

With tears in her eyes that I had never expected to see, Christina rushed forward and threw her arms around his neck. 'Oh, Father, let's leave the past to mend itself and go home.'

With their old family loyalties still intact, Kildennan, his daughter, and his men turned their backs on us and walked silently away, leading the stallion along behind them. They disappeared into the mist like the phantoms of some vanished Jacobite army.

'Archie!'

It was a cry of sheer joy that burst from Janet's lips when she saw her husband and Leithen emerge from the trees. She flung herself onto him with a wild embrace that set him laughing uncontrollably.

'Steady on, old girl! People are watching.'

'Let them!' Janet planted a kiss full on his lips then took a small step back with her hands resting on his shoulders. 'You magnificent fool! Don't you ever try to leave me behind again.'

'We couldn't see much through this drizzle,' said Leithen, 'but it looked as though the armistice had arrived.'

'Yes, Ned,' I agreed, 'it seems John Macnab has pulled it off again.'

Prince Edward glanced up at the castle. 'I'd better go up there and have a word with the old boy. I'm sure he must be in the most frightful state.'

He set off up the crag with Creevey following closely behind.

'Speaking of John Macnab,' said Leithen, 'whatever's become of the rest of our crew?'

As if in answer to his question, the roar of an engine heralded the arrival of a military motorcycle. It bumped over the rocky ground and halted in front of us. Lamancha pushed up his goggles and grinned.

'What's up, chaps? Have we missed all the fun?'.

Palliser-Yeates appeared grateful to be able to climb down from behind and rub his bruised rear.

'Charles, I shall never get on one of those machines again so long as I live. In fact it may be some time before I can even sit down.'

'You know, I've always rather fancied getting one of these for myself,' said Archie, admiring the bike.

'Where on earth did you get it?' I asked.

'And what in heaven's name have you been up to?' added Leithen.

Lamancha dismounted and took a swig of whisky from his hip flask.

'Well, we were having a jolly set-to with Baron von Hilderling's mob, bullets flying and whatnot, when a squad of Seaforth Highlanders showed up and arrested the whole bunch of us. We were bundled off to Fort Donald for the night. Luckily General Torrance is an old friend of my father's, so we were able to patch things up without too much trouble.'

'The general's sent Hilderling and his gang off under armed escort,' said Palliser-Yeates, 'to be put aboard the first steamer back to Germany.'

'After that he let me borrow this fine machine so we could come looking for you fellows,' Lamancha concluded. 'I expect you've got quite a tale of your own to tell.'

'We do,' I said, 'but that can wait until we're somewhere warm and dry with a good supper in front of us.'

24

THE FIELDS OF GOLD

———

Once we got Wilhelm settled into a bed at Rushforth Lodge, Prince Edward and Creevey made a discreet departure. Janet had left the ever reliable Stokes with instructions to restock the larder, so we were treated to prodigious quantities of roast chicken, game pie, and smoked salmon, all washed down with ample amounts of Bordeaux wine. This was followed by a platter of cheeses and a selection of malt whiskies.

Once he was sure his master was peacefully sleeping off the effects of his trial, Captain von Ilsemann joined us to exchange tales of our adventures past and present. Several toasts were offered to Janet as the Queen of the Feast, for there was no doubt in any of our minds that it was she who had saved the day.

In the morning Leithen and I borrowed the Hispana to drive the Kaiser and his adjutant to Barrastane, where curving granite cliffs formed a natural harbour. An elegant schooner was anchored there, bright blue and yellow with polished brass fittings. Following an exchange of signals between Ilsemann, standing on the clifftop, and a crewman on the deck below, a dinghy was launched to collect the returning passengers from the beach.

The Kaiser, recovered from the rigours of the last few days, now stood before us, a figure of undaunted pride. It was almost possible to see how, with a little more wisdom and humanity, he might have become a monarch worthy of his high station.

'Gentlemen, you have done me a great service,' he told us with stiff formality. 'I shall not forget that.'

He saluted us as though we were soldiers passing before him on parade. Reflexively Leithen and I returned the salute and watched him walk to the steps that led down the cliff face to the beach.

Ilsemann lingered long enough to shake hands with both of us.

'Sir Richard, Sir Edward, once we were enemies on the field of battle, but today I am proud to call you allies and friends. It is quite clear that the British Tommy has lost none of his – what did Sir Archie call it? – *pluck*.'

'It usually comes out when our backs are to the wall,' I said, smiling at the genuine warmth of his words. 'It is just as evident that the decent German officer has lost none of his gallantry.'

'But please,' Leithen added, 'make sure that your emperor never again sets out on such a damned fool venture.'

'After this experience,' said Ilsemann, 'I believe he will be content to sit comfortably at home and write his memoirs.'

With a final exchange of salutes, he followed his master down to the beach. Once the dinghy had transferred them to the schooner, they set sail for the open sea.

The sky was still overcast and I could not escape the ever present sense of an impending storm as I watched the vessel fade away into the hazy distance.

'Have we achieved anything here, Ned?' I wondered.

'We've kept the hand of a grief-stricken man from murder, and that's worth something,' my friend replied.

'But will the war return in spite of all our efforts? It hardly bears thinking about.'

After a pensive moment Leithen said, 'I don't doubt there are hard times ahead and we'll face them as we always have. But I believe that in the long run the old world will pull through and everything we've fought and sacrificed for will finally unfold like fields of gold beneath a fresher sun.'

At that instant the clouds parted and a wash of sunshine dashed over the cliff face to our left, transfiguring it into a lofty wall of shimmering white marble brightly veined with silver and emerald green. Rising above this rampart, the rocky crags, flickering with honeyed light, were transformed into the towers of a fabulous palace, while streamers of white mist fluttered over them like banners.

I swallowed hard and glanced at Leithen. I could tell that he too beheld the very same vision that had just burst upon my astonished eyes. Even as the clouds closed over the sun and the cliff face darkened once more to grey, I knew what it was that we had seen.

One day we would meet there at the gates of that city.

EPILOGUE

'What you have come to is nothing known to the senses: not a blazing fire, or a gloom turning to total darkness, or a storm; or trumpeting thunder or the great voice speaking which made everyone that heard it beg that no more should be said to them. But what you have come to is Mount Zion and the city of the living God, the heavenly Jerusalem where the millions of angels have gathered for the festival, with the whole Church in which everyone is a first-born son and a citizen of Heaven.'

HEBREWS: XII 18–19, 22–23

AUTHOR'S NOTE

Following his abdication in 1918 the former Kaiser Wilhelm II lived in exile in Holland until his death in 1941. When the Nazi armies invaded Holland in 1940 the British royal family offered him refuge in the UK. He declined their invitation.

I gained much valuable information from Lady Norah Bentinck's fascinating book *The Ex-Kaiser In Exile* (1921), in which she describes her meetings with the exiled monarch and the members of his household. Captain von Ilsemann's views on the war and the Kaiser's less palatable obsessions are all a matter of record.

Many thanks as ever must go to my wife Debby for all her work on this project and to my indefatigable researcher Kirsty Nicoll. My friend Steve Johnston took me fly fishing and clay pigeon shooting in order to make a proper Macnab out of me. Thanks also to Hugh Raven, who treated Debby and me to a wonderful few days on his Ardtornish estate where we tramped through the hills with our dog Kyra. Many of our experiences in that beautiful landscape have found their way into this book.

As well as taking inspiration from the classic *John Macnab*, I have also borrowed the characters of Warren Creevey and Baron von Hilderling from John Buchan's later novel *A Prince of the Captivity* (1933).

For more information on *Castle Macnab*, *The Thirty-One Kings* and my other projects, please visit my website www.harris-authors.com.

R.J.H.